Predictable. That was what taking Sabine to bed should have been.

So why had it been so totally, utterly not the way he'd predicted? That was what he wanted to know. Not just wanted—*needed* to know.

Memories flooded through Bastiaan, hot and overwhelming, of just how he had responded to her as he'd held her in his arms. How the consummation of their congress had been like nothing he'd ever experienced before!

As if she is the only woman in the world! The only woman in the world for me.

He fought it down. Harshly, vehemently. This was Sabine he was talking about! Sabine, in whom he had absolutely no interest whatsoever except that of getting her claws out of Philip by any means available. And the means he had selected were intended to achieve that end and simultaneously— conveniently!—allow him to slake his lust for her.

Yet here he was, shaken by the memory of the night, staring out over the ocean and wondering what the hell had gone wrong with his plan.

Julia James lives in England and adores the peaceful, verdant countryside and the wild shores of Cornwall. She also loves the Mediterranean—so rich in myth and history, with its sunbaked landscapes and olive groves, ancient ruins and azure seas. "The perfect setting for romance!" she says. "Rivaled only by the lush tropical heat of the Caribbean—palms swaying by a silver sand beach lapped by turquoise waters...what more could lovers want?"

Books by Julia James

Harlequin Presents

Captivated by the Greek
The Forbidden Touch of Sanguardo
Securing the Greek's Legacy
Painted the Other Woman
The Dark Side of Desire
From Dirt to Diamonds
Forbidden or For Bedding?
Penniless and Purchased
The Greek's Million-Dollar Baby Bargain
Greek Tycoon, Waitress Wife
The Italian's Rags-to-Riches Wife
Bedded, or Wedded?

Visit the Author Profile page
at Harlequin.com for more titles.

Julia James

A TYCOON TO BE RECKONED WITH

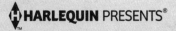
HARLEQUIN PRESENTS®

Recycling programs
for this product may
not exist in your area.

ISBN-13: 978-0-373-13437-3

A Tycoon to Be Reckoned With

First North American Publication 2016

Copyright © 2016 by Julia James

Printed in U.S.A.

A TYCOON TO BE
RECKONED WITH

For IHV, who gave me my love of opera.

CHAPTER ONE

'You know, it's you I blame.'

Bastiaan's aunt tried to laugh as she spoke, but it was shaky, Bastiaan could tell.

'It was you who suggested Philip go and stay in your villa at Cap Pierre!'

Bastiaan took the criticism on board. 'I thought it might help—moving him out of target range to finish his university vacation assignments in peace and quiet.'

His aunt sighed. 'Alas, it seems he has jumped out of the frying pan into the fire. He may have escaped Elena Constantis, but this female in France sounds infinitely worse.'

Bastiaan's dark eyes took on a mordant expression. 'Unfortunately, wherever in the world Philip is he will be a target.'

'If only he were less sweet-natured. If he had your... *toughness*,' Bastiaan's aunt replied, her gaze falling on her nephew.

'I'll take that as a compliment,' Bastiaan replied dryly. 'But Philip will toughen up, don't worry.' *He'll need to*, he thought caustically. Just as he himself had had to.

'He's so impressionable!' his aunt cried. 'And so handsome. No wonder these wretched girls make a beeline for him.'

And, of course, so rich, Bastiaan added cynically—but silently. No point worrying his already anxious aunt further. It was Philip's wealth—the wealth he would be inheriting from his late father's estate once he turned twenty-one in a couple of months—that would attract females far more dangerous than the merely irksome spoilt teenage princess Elena Constantis. The real danger would come from a very different type of female.

Call them what one liked—and Bastiaan had several names not suitable for his aunt's ears—the most universal name was a familiar one: gold-diggers. Females who took one look at his young, good-looking, impressionable and soon to be very rich cousin and licked their lips in anticipation.

That was the problem right now. A woman who appeared to be licking her lips over Philip. And the danger was, Bastiaan knew, very real. For Philip, so Paulette, his housekeeper at Cap Pierre, had informed him, far from diligently writing his essays, had taken to haunting the nearby town of Pierre-les-Pins and a venue there that was most undesirable for a twenty-year-old. Apparently attracted by an even more undesirable female working there.

'A singer in a nightclub!' his aunt wailed now. 'I cannot believe Philip would fall for a woman like that!'

'It *is* something of a cliché…' Bastiaan allowed.

His aunt bridled. 'A cliché? Bastiaan, is that all you have to say about it?'

He shook his head. 'No. I could say a great deal more—but to what purpose?' Bastiaan got to his feet. He was of an imposing height, standing well over six feet, and powerfully built. 'Don't worry…' he made his voice reassuring now '… I'll deal with it. Philip will *not* be sacrificed to a greedy woman's ambitions.'

His aunt stood up, clutching at his sleeve. *'Thank you,'* she said. 'I knew I could count on you.' Her eyes misted a little. 'Take care of my darling boy, Bastiaan. He has no father now to look out for him.'

Bastiaan pressed his aunt's hand sympathetically. His maternal uncle had succumbed to heart disease when Philip had just started at university, and he knew how hard her husband's death had hit his aunt. Knew, too, with a shadowing of his eyes, how losing a father too young—as he himself had when not much older than Philip—left a void.

'I'll keep Philip safe, I promise you,' he assured his aunt now, as she took her leave.

He saw her to her car, watched it head down the driveway of his property in the affluent outskirts of Athens. Then he went back indoors, his mouth tightening.

His aunt's fears were not groundless. Until Philip turned twenty-one Bastiaan was his trustee—overseeing all his finances, managing his investments—while Philip enjoyed a more than generous allowance to cover his personal spending. Usually Bastiaan did nothing more than cast a casual eye over the bank and credit card statements, but an unusually large amount—twenty thousand euros—had gone out in a single payment a week ago. The cheque had been paid into an unknown personal account at the Nice branch of a French bank. There was no reason—no *good* reason—that Bastiaan could come up with for such a transfer. There was, however, one very bad reason for it—and that he *could* come up with.

The gold-digger had already started taking gold from the mine....

Bastiaan's features darkened. The sooner he disposed of this nightclub singer who was making eyes at his cousin—and his cousin's fortune—the better. He headed purposefully to his study. If he was to leave for France in the morning, he had work to do tonight. Enterprises with portfolios the size of Karavalas did not run themselves. His cousin's fortune might be predominantly in the form of blue chip stocks, but Bastiaan preferred to diversify across a broad range of investment opportunities, from industry and property to entrepreneurial start-ups. But, for all their variety, they all shared one aspect in common—they all made him money. A *lot* of money.

The cynical curve was back at Bastiaan's mouth as he sat himself down behind his desk and flicked on his PC. He'd told his aunt that her son would toughen up in time—and he knew from his own experience that that was true. Memory glinted in his dark eyes.

When his own father had died, he'd assuaged his grief by partying hard and extravagantly, with no paternal guardian to moderate his excesses. The spree had ended abruptly. He'd been in a casino, putting away the champagne and generally flashing his cash lavishly, and it had promptly lured across a female—Leana—who had been all over him. At just twenty-three he'd been happy to enjoy all she'd offered him—the company of her luscious body in bed included. So much so that when she'd fed him some story of how she'd stupidly got herself into debt with the casino and was worried sick about it, he'd grandly handed her a more than handsome cheque, feeling munificent and generous towards the beautiful, sexy woman who'd seemed so keen on him...

She'd disappeared the day the cheque had cleared—heading off, so he'd heard, on a yacht belonging to a seventy-year-old Mexican millionaire, never to be seen again by Bastiaan. He'd been royally fleeced and proved to be a complete mug. It had stung, no doubt about it, but he'd learnt his lesson, all right—an expensive one. It wasn't one he wanted Philip to learn the same way. Apart from taking a large wedge of his money, Leana had damaged his self-esteem—an uncomfortably sobering experience for his younger self. Although it had made him wise up decisively.

But, unlike Bastiaan, Philip was of a romantic disposition, and a gold-digging seductress might wound him more deeply than just in his wallet and his self-esteem. That was not something Bastiaan would permit. After his experience with Leana he'd become wise to the wiles women threw out to him, and sceptical of their apparent devotion. Now, into his thirties, he knew they considered him a tough nut—ruthless, even...

His eyes hardened beneath dark brows. That was something this ambitious nightclub singer would soon discover for herself.

Sarah stood motionless on the low stage, the spotlight on her, while her audience beyond, sitting at their tables, mostly continued their conversations as they ate and drank.

I'm just a divertimento, she thought to herself, acidly. *Background music.* She nodded at Max on the piano, throat muscles ready, and he played the opening to her number. It was easy and low-pitched, making no demands on her upper register. It was just as well—the last thing she wanted to do was risk her voice singing in this smoky atmosphere.

As she sang the first bars her breasts lifted, making her all too aware of just how low-cut the bodice of her champagne satin gown was. Her long hair was swept over one bare shoulder. It was, she knew, a stereotypical 'vamp' image—the sultry nightclub singer with her slinky dress, low-pitched voice, over-made-up eyes and long blonde locks.

She tensed instinctively. Well, that was the idea, wasn't it? To stand in for the club's missing resident *chanteuse,* Sabine Sablon, who had abruptly vacated the role when she'd run off with a rich customer without warning.

It hadn't been Sarah's idea to take over as Sabine, but Max had been blunt about it. If she didn't agree to sing here in the evenings, then Raymond, the nightclub owner, lacking a *chanteuse*, would refuse to let Max have the run of the place during the day. And without that they couldn't rehearse…and without rehearsals they couldn't appear at the Provence en Voix music festival.

And if they didn't appear there her last chance would be gone.

My last chance—my last chance to achieve my dream!

Her dream of breaking through from being just one more of the scores upon scores of hopeful, aspiring sopranos who crowded the operatic world, all desperate to make their mark. If she could not succeed now, she would have to abandon the dream that had possessed her since her teenage years, and all the way through music college and the tough, ultra-competitive world beyond as she'd struggled to make herself heard by those who could lift her from the crowd and launch her career.

She'd tried so hard, for so long, and now she was on the wrong side of twenty-five, racing towards thirty, with time against her and younger singers coming up behind her. Everything rested on this final attempt—and if it failed… Well, then, she would accept defeat. Resign herself to teaching instead. It was the way she was currently earning her living, part-time at a school in her native Yorkshire, though she found it unfulfilling, craving the excitement and elation of performing live.

So not yet—*oh, not yet*—would she give up on her dreams. Not until she'd put everything into this music festival, singing the soprano lead in what she knew could only be a high-risk gamble: a newly written opera by an unknown composer, performed by unknown singers, all on a shoestring. A shoestring that Max, their fanatically driven director and conductor, was already stretching to the utmost. Everything, but *everything*, was being done on a tiny budget, with savings being made wherever they could. Including rehearsal space.

So every night bar Sundays, she had to become Sabine Sablon, husking away into the microphone, drawing male eyes all around. It was not a comfortable feeling—and it was a million miles away from her true self. Max could tell her all he liked that it would give her valuable insight into roles such as *La Traviata*'s courtesan Violetta, or the coquettish Manon, but on an operatic stage everyone would know she was simply playing a part. Here, everyone looking at her really thought she *was* Sabine Sablon.

A silent shudder went through her. Dear God, if anyone in the opera world found out she was singing here, like this, her credibility would be shot to pieces. No one would take her seriously for a moment.

And neither Violetta nor Manon was anything like her role in Anton's opera *War Bride.* Her character was a romantic young girl, falling in love with a dashing soldier. A whirlwind courtship, a return to the front—and then the dreaded news of her husband's fate. The heartbreak of loss and bereavement. And then a child born to take his father's place in yet another war…

The simple, brutal tale was told as a timeless fable of the sacrifice and futility of war, repeated down the ages, its score haunting and poignant. It had captivated Sarah the first moment she'd heard Max play it.

What must it be like to love so swiftly, to hurt so badly? she'd wondered as she'd started to explore her role. For herself, she had no knowledge—had never experienced the heady whirlwind of love nor the desolation of heartbreak. Her only serious relationship had ended last year when Andrew, a cellist she had known since college, had been offered a place in a prestigious orchestra in Germany. It had been his breakthrough moment, and she had been so glad for him—had waved him off without a thought of holding him back.

Both of them had always known that their careers must come first in their lives, which meant that neither could afford to invest in a deeply emotional relationship which might jeopardise their diverging career paths. So neither had grieved when they'd parted, only wished each other well. Theirs had been a relationship based primarily on a shared passion for music, rather than for each other—friendship and affection had bound them, nothing more than that.

But this meant she knew that in order to portray her character now—the War Bride—as convincingly as she could, she would need to call on all her imagination. Just as she would need all her operatic abilities to do credit to the challenging vocal demands of the hauntingly beautiful but technically difficult music.

She reached the end of her song to a smattering of applause. Dipping her head in acknowledgement, she shifted her weight from one high-heeled foot to the other. As she straightened again, sending her gaze back out over the dining area, she felt a sudden flickering awareness go through her. She could hear Max start the introduction to her next number but ignored it, her senses suddenly on alert. She heard him repeat the phrase, caught him glancing at her with a frown, but her attention was not on him—not on the song she was supposed to have started four bars earlier. Her attention was on the audience beyond.

Someone was looking at her. Someone standing at the back of the room.

He had not been there a moment ago and must have just come in. She shook her head, trying to dismiss that involuntary sense of heightened awareness, of sudden exposure. Male eyes gazed at her all the time—and there was always movement beyond the stage…diners and waiters. They did not make her pause the way this had—as if there were something different about him. She wanted to see him more clearly, but the light was wrong and he was too far away for her to discern anything more than a tall, tuxedo-clad figure at the back of the room.

For the third time she heard Max repeat the intro—insistently this time. And she knew she had to start to sing. Not just because of Max's impatient prompt but because she suddenly, urgently, needed to do something other than simply stand there, pooled in the light that emphasised every slender curve of her tightly sheathed body. Exposed her to that invisible yet almost tangible scrutiny that was palpable in its impact on her.

As she started the number her voice was more husky than ever. Her long, artificial lashes swept down over her deeply kohled eyes, and the sweep of her hair dipped halfway across her jawline and cheekbone. She forced herself to keep singing, to try and suppress the frisson of disturbed awareness that was tensing through her—the sense of being the object of attention that was like a beam targeted at her.

Somehow she got through to the end of the number, pulling herself together to start the next one on time and not fluff it. It seemed easier now, and she realised that at some point that sense of being under scrutiny had faded and dissipated. As if a kind of pressure had been lifted off her. She reached the end of the last number, the end of her set, with a sense of relief. She made her way off-stage, hearing canned music starting up and Max closing down the piano.

One of the waiters intercepted her. 'There's a guy who wants to buy you a drink,' he said.

Sarah made a face. It wasn't unusual that this happened, but she never accepted.

The waiter held up a hundred-euro note. 'Looks like he's keen,' he informed her with a lift of his brow.

'Well, he's the only one who is,' she said. 'Better take it back to him,' she added. 'I don't want him thinking I pocketed it and then didn't show.'

Her refusal got Max's approval. 'No time for picking up men,' he said, flippantly but pointedly.

'As if I would…' She rolled her eyes.

For a moment, it crossed her mind that the invitation to buy her a drink might be connected to that shadowy figure at the back of the room and his disturbing perusal of her, but then she dismissed the thought. All she wanted to do now was get out of her costume and head for bed. Max started opera rehearsals promptly every morning, and she needed to sleep.

She'd just reached her dressing room, kicking off her high heels and flexing her feet in relief, when there was a brief knock at the door. She only had time to say, 'Who is it?' before the door opened.

She glanced up, assuming it would be Max, wanting to tell her something that couldn't wait. But instead it was a man she'd never seen before in her life.

And he stilled the breath in her lungs.

CHAPTER TWO

BASTIAAN'S EYES ZEROED in on the figure seated at the brightly lit vanity unit with its trademark light-bulb-surrounded mirror. Backlit as she was by the high-wattage bulbs, her face was in shadow.

But the shadows did nothing to dim her impact. If anything it emphasised it, casting her features into relief. On stage, she'd been illuminated in a pool of light, her features softened by the distance at which he'd sat. He'd deliberately taken a table at the rear of the room, wanting at that point only to observe without being noticed in return.

It hadn't taken him more than two moments to realise that the female poised on the stage possessed a quality that signalled danger to his young, impressionable cousin.

Allure—it was an old-fashioned word, but that was the one that had come to his mind as his eyes had rested on the slender figure sensuously draped in low-cut clinging satin, standing in a pool of soft, smoky light, her fingers lightly curved around her microphone, the lustrous fall of her long blonde hair curled over her bare shoulder like a vamp from the forties.

Her mouth was painted a rich, luscious red, her eye make-up was pronounced, with long, artificial lashes framing luminous eyes. Seeing her now, close up, she was even more alluring.

No wonder Philip is smitten!

His eyes completed his swift scrutiny and he was interested to see a line of colour running along her cheekbones. *Curious…* he thought. Then the tightening of her mouth told him what had accounted for that reaction. It was not a blush—a woman like her probably hadn't blushed since puberty—it was annoyance.

Why? he found himself wondering. Women were not usually annoyed when he paid them attention. Quite the reverse. But this *chanteuse* was. It was doubly unusual because surely a woman in her profession was well used to male admirers courting her in her dressing room.

An unwelcome thought crossed his mind—was it his cousin's wont to hang out here? Did she invite him to her changing room?

Just how far has she got with him?

Well, however far it was, it was going to stop from now on. Whatever story she'd trotted out to Philip in order to get him to give her money, the gold mine was closing down…

She was looking at him still, that scarlet mouth of hers pressed tightly, and something sparking now in her eyes.

'Oui?' she said pointedly.

His eyelids dipped over his eyes briefly. 'Did the waiter not pass on my invitation?' he asked, speaking in French, which he spoke as well as English and a couple of other languages as well.

Her arched eyebrows rose. 'It was you?' she said. Then, without bothering to wait for a reply, she simply went on, 'I'm afraid I don't accept invitations to share a drink with any of the club's guests.'

Her tone was dismissive, and Bastiaan felt a flicker

of annoyance at it. Dismissive was not the kind of voice he was used to hearing in women he was speaking to. Or indeed from anyone he was speaking to. And in someone whose career relied on the attention and appreciation of others, it was out of place.

Perhaps she thinks she does not need to court her audience any longer? Perhaps she thinks she already has a very comfortable exit from her profession lined up?

The flicker of annoyance sparked to something sharper. But he did not let it show. Not now—not yet. At the moment, his aim was to disarm her. Defeating her would come afterwards.

'Then allow me to invite you to dinner instead,' he responded. Deliberately, he infused a subtly caressing note into his voice that he'd found successful at any other time he'd chosen to adopt it.

That line of colour ran out over her cheekbones again. But this time there was no accompanying tightening of her red mouth. Instead she gave a brief smile. It was civil only—nothing more than that, Bastiaan could see.

'Thank you, but no. And now...' the smile came again, and he could see that her intention was to terminate the exchange '...if you will excuse me, I must get changed.' She paused expectantly, waiting for him to withdraw.

He ignored the prompt. Instead one eyebrow tilted interrogatively. 'You have another dinner engagement?' he asked.

Something snapped in her eyes, changing their colour, he noticed. He'd assumed they were a shade of grey, but suddenly there was a flash of green in them.

'No,' she said precisely. 'And if I did, *m'sieu*—' the pointedness was back in her voice now '—I don't believe it would be any of your concern.' She smiled tightly, with less civility now.

If it were with my cousin, mademoiselle, it would indeed be my concern... That flicker of more than annoyance came again, but again Bastiaan concealed it.

'In which case, what can be your objection to dining with me?' Again, there was the same note in his voice that worked so well with women in general. Invitations to dine with him had never, in his living memory, been met with rejection.

She was staring at him with those eyes that had gone back to grey now, the flash of green quite absent. Eyes that were outlined in black kohl, their sockets dramatised outrageously with make-up, their lashes doubled in length by artificial means and copious mascara.

Staring at him in a way he'd never been stared at before.

As though she didn't quite believe what she was seeing. Or hearing.

For just a second their eyes met, and then, as if in recoil, her fake lashes dropped down over her eyes, veiling them.

She took a breath. '*M'sieu*, I am desolated to inform you that I also do not accept invitations to dine with the club's guests,' she said. She didn't make her tone dismissive now, but absolute.

He ignored it. 'I wasn't thinking of dining here,' he said. 'I would prefer to take you to Le Tombleur,' he murmured.

Her eyes widened just a fraction. Le Tombleur was currently the most fashionable restaurant on the Côte D'Azur, and Bastiaan was sure that the chance to dine at such a fabulous locale would surely stop her prevaricating in this fashion. It would also, he knew, set her mind instantly at rest as to whether he was someone possessed of sufficient financial means to be of interest to her. She would not wish to waste her time on someone who was not in the same league as his young cousin. Had she but known, Bastiaan thought cynically, his own fortune was considerably greater than Philip's.

But of course Philip's fortune was far more accessible to her. Or might be. If she were truly setting Philip in her sightline, she would be cautious about switching her attentions elsewhere—it would lose her Philip if he discovered it.

A thought flickered across Bastiaan's mind. She was alluring enough—even for himself... Should *that* be his method of detaching her? Then he dismissed it. Of course he would not be involving himself in any kind of liaison with a woman such as this one. However worthy the intention.

Dommage... He heard the French word in his head. *What a pity*...

'*M'sieu*...' She was speaking again, with razored precision. 'As I say, I must decline your very...*generous*... invitation'.

Had there been a twist in her phrasing of the word 'generous'? An ironic inflection indicating that she had formed an opinion of him that was not the one he'd intended her to form?

He felt a new emotion flicker within him like a low-voltage electric current.

Could there possibly be more to this woman sitting there, looking up at him through those absurdly fake eyelashes, with a strange expression in her grey-green eyes—more green now than grey, he realised. His awareness of that colour-change was of itself distracting, and it made his own eyes narrow assessingly.

For just a fraction of a second their eyes seemed to

meet, and Bastiaan felt the voltage of the electric current surging within him.

'Are you ready to go yet?'

A different voice interjected, coming from the door, which had been pushed wider by a man—a youngish one—clad in a dinner jacket, half leaning his slightly built body against the doorjamb. The man had clearly addressed Sabine, but now, registering that there was someone else in her dressing room, his eyes went to Bastiaan.

He frowned, about to say something, but Sabine Sablon interjected. 'The gentleman is just leaving,' she announced.

Her voice was cool, but Bastiaan was too experienced with women not to know that she was not, in fact, as composed as she wanted to appear. And he knew what was causing it...

Satisfaction soared through him. Oh, this sultry, sophisticated *chanteuse*, with her vampish allure, her skin-tight dress and over-made-up face, might be appearing as cool as the proverbial cucumber—but that flash in her eyes had told him that however resistant she appeared to be to his overtures, an appearance was all it was...

I can reach her. She is vulnerable to me.

That was the truth she'd so unguardedly—so unwisely—just revealed to him.

He changed his stance. Glanced at the man hovering in the doorway. A slight sense of familiarity assailed him, and a moment later he knew why. He was the accompanist for the *chanteuse*.

For a fleeting moment he found himself speculating on whether the casual familiarity he could sense between the two of them betokened a more intimate relationship. Then he rejected it. Every male instinct told him that whatever lover the accompanist took would not be female.

Bastiaan's sense of satisfaction increased, and his annoyance with the intruder decreased proportionately. He turned his attention back to his quarry.

'I shall take my leave, then, *mademoiselle*,' he said, and he did not trouble to hide his ironic inflection or his amusement. Dark, dangerous amusement. As though her rejection of him was clearly nothing more than a feminine ploy—one he was seeing through...but currently choosing to indulge. He gave the slightest nod of his head, the slightest sardonic smile.

'*A bientôt.*'

Then, paying not the slightest attention to the accompanist, who had to straighten to let him pass, he walked out.

As he left he heard the *chanteuse* exclaim, 'Thank goodness you rescued me!'

Bastiaan could hear the relief in her tone. His satisfaction went up yet another level. A tremor—a discernible tremor—had been audible in her voice. That was good.

Yes, she is vulnerable to me.

He walked on down the corridor, casually letting himself out through the rear entrance into the narrow roadway beyond, before walking around to the front of the club, where his car was parked on the forecourt. Lowering himself into its low-slung frame, he started the engine, its low, throaty growl echoing the silent growl inside his head.

'*Thank goodness you rescued me!*' she had said, this harpy who was trying to extract his cousin's fortune from him.

Bastiaan's mouth thinned to a tight, narrow line, his eyes hardening as he headed out on to the road, setting his route back towards Monaco, where he was staying tonight in the duplex apartment he kept there.

Well, in that she was mistaken—most decidedly.

No one will rescue you from me.

Of that he was certain.

He drove on into the night.

'Give me two minutes and I'll be ready to go,' Sarah said.

She strove for composure, but felt as if she'd just been released from a seizure of her senses that had crushed the breath from her lungs. How she'd managed to keep her cool she had no idea—she had only know that keeping her cool was absolutely essential.

What the hell had just happened to her? Out of nowhere…the way it had?

That had been the man whose assessing gaze she'd picked up during her final number. She'd been able to feel it from right across the club—and when he'd walked into her dressing room it had been like…

Like nothing I've ever known. Nothing I've ever felt—

Never before had a man had such a raw, physical impact on her. Hitting her senses like a sledgehammer. She tried to analyse it now—needing to do so. His height, towering over her in the tiny dressing room, had dominated the encounter. The broad shoulders had been sleekly clad in a bespoke dinner jacket, and there had been an impression of power that she had derived not just from the clearly muscular physique he possessed but by an aura about him that had told her this man was used to getting his own way.

Especially with women.

Because it hadn't just been the clear impression that here was a wealthy man who could buy female favours—his mention of Le Tombleur had been adequate demonstration of *that*—it had been far, far more…

She felt herself swallow. *He doesn't need money to impress women.*

No, she acknowledged shakily, all it took was those piercing dark eyes, winged with darker brows, the strong blade of his nose, the wide, sensual curve of his mouth and the tough line of his jaw.

He was a man who knew perfectly well that his appeal to women was powerful—who knew perfectly well that women responded to him on that account.

She felt her hackles rise automatically.

He thought I'd jump at the chance!

A rush of weakness swept through her. Thank God she'd had the presence of mind—pulled urgently out of her reeling senses—to react the way she'd managed to do.

What was it about him that he should have had such an effect on me?

Just what had it been about that particular combination of physique, looks and sheer, raw personal impact that had made her react as if she were a sliver of steel in the sudden presence of a magnetic field so strong it had made the breath still in her body?

She had seen better-looking men in her time, but not a single one had ever had the raw, visceral, overpowering impact on her senses that this man had. Even in the space of a few charged minutes…

She shook her head again, trying to clear the image from her mind. Whoever he was, he'd gone.

As she got on with the task of turning herself back into Sarah, shedding the false eyelashes, heavy make-up and tight satin gown, she strove to dismiss him from her thoughts. *Put him out of your head*, she told herself brusquely. *It was Sabine Sablon he wanted to invite to dinner, not Sarah Fareham.*

That was the truth of it, she knew. Sabine was the

kind of woman a man like that would be interested in—sophisticated, seductive, a woman of the world, a *femme fatale*. And she wasn't Sabine—she most definitely was not. So it was completely irrelevant that she'd reacted to the man the way she had.

I haven't got time to be bowled over by some arrogantly smouldering alpha male who thinks he's picking up a sultry woman like Sabine. However much he knocked me sideways.

She had one focus in her life right now—only one. And it was *not* a man with night-dark eyes and devastating looks who sucked the breath from her body.

She headed out to where Max was waiting to walk her back to her *pension*, some blocks away in this harbourside *ville* of Pierre-les-Pins, before carrying on to the apartment he shared with Anton, the opera's composer.

As they set off he launched into speech without preamble. 'I've been thinking,' he said, 'in your first duet with Alain—'

And he was off, instructing her in some troublesome vocal technicalities he wanted to address at the next day's rehearsal. Sarah was glad, for it helped to distance her mind from that brief but disturbing encounter in her dressing room with that devastating, dangerous man.

Dangerous? The word echoed in her head, taking her aback. *Had* he been dangerous? Truly?

She gave herself a mental shake. She was being absurd. How could a complete stranger be dangerous to her? Of course he couldn't.

It was absurd to think so.

CHAPTER THREE

'BASTIAAN! FANTASTIC! I'd no idea you were here in France!' Philip's voice was warm and enthusiastic as he answered his mobile.

'Monaco, to be precise,' Bastiaan answered, strolling with his phone to the huge plate-glass window of his high-rise apartment in Monte Carlo, which afforded a panoramic view over the harbour, chock-full of luxury yachts glittering in the morning sunshine.

'But you'll come over to the villa, won't you?' his cousin asked eagerly.

'Seeking distraction from your essays…?' Bastiaan trailed off deliberately, knowing the boy had distraction already—a dangerous one.

As it had done ever since he'd left the nightclub last night, the seductive image of Sabine Sablon slid into his inner vision. Enough to distract anyone. Even himself…

He pulled his mind away. Time to discover just how deep Philip was with the alluring *chanteuse*. 'Well,' he continued, 'I can be with you within the hour if you like?'

He did not get an immediate reply. Then Philip was saying, 'Could you make it a bit later than that?'

'Studying so hard?' Bastiaan asked lightly.

'Well, not precisely. I mean, I *am*—I've got one essay

nearly finished—but actually, I'm a bit tied up till lunch-time…'

Philip's voice trailed off, and Bastiaan could hear the constraint in his cousin's voice. He was hiding something.

Deliberately, Bastiaan backed off. 'No problem,' he said. 'See you for lunch, then—around one… Is that OK?' He paused. 'Do you want me to tell Paulette to expect me, or will you?'

'Would *you*?' said Philip, from which Bastiaan drew his own conclusion. Philip wasn't at the villa right now.

'No problem,' he said again, making his voice easy still. Easier than his mind…

So, if Philip wasn't struggling with his history essays at the villa, where was he?

Is he with her now?

He could feel his hackles rising down his spine. Was that why she had turned down dining with him at Le Tombleur? Because she'd been about to rendezvous with his cousin? Had Philip spent the night with her?

A growl started in his throat. Philip might be legally free to have a relationship with anyone he wanted, but even if the *chanteuse* had been as pure as the driven snow, with the financial probity of a nun, she was utterly unsuitable for a first romance for a boy his age. She was nearer thirty than twenty…

'Great!' Philip was saying now. 'See you then, Bast—gotta go.'

The call was disconnected and Bastiaan dropped his phone back in his pocket slowly, staring out of the window. Multi-million-pound yachts crowded the marina, and the fairy tale royal palace looked increasingly be-sieged by the high-rise buildings that maximised the tiny footprint of the principality.

He turned away. His apartment here had been an excellent investment, and the rental income was exceptional during the Monaco Grand Prix, but Monte Carlo was not his favourite place. He far preferred his villa on Cap Pierre, where Philip was staying. Better still, his own private island off the Greek west coast. That was where he went when he truly wanted to be himself. One day he'd take the woman who would be his wife there—the woman he would spend the rest of his life with.

Although just who she would be he had no idea. His experience with women was wide, indeed, but so far not one of his many female acquaintances had come anywhere close to tempting him to make a relationship with her permanent. One thing he was sure of—when he met her, he'd know she was the one.

There'd be no mistaking that.

Meantime he'd settle himself down at the dining table, open his laptop and get some work done before heading off to meet Philip—and finding out just how bad his infatuation was…

'I could murder a coffee.' Sarah, dismissed by Max for now, while he focussed his attentions on the small chorus, plonked herself down at the table near the front of the stage where Philip was sitting.

He'd become a fixture at their rehearsals, and Sarah hadn't the heart to discourage him. He was a sweet guy, Philip Markiotis, and he had somehow attached himself to the little opera company in the role of unofficial runner—fetching coffee, refilling water jugs, copying scores, helping tidy up after rehearsals.

And all the time, Sarah thought with a softening of her expression, he was carrying a youthful torch for her that glowed in every yearning glance that came her way. He was only a few years older than her own sixth-formers, and his admiration for her must remain hopeless, but she would never dream of hurting his feelings. She knew how very real they seemed to him.

Memory sifted through Sarah's head. She knew what Philip was experiencing. OK, she could laugh at herself now, but as a music student she'd had *the* most lovestruck crush on the tenor who'd taken a summer master class she'd attended. She'd been totally smitten, unable to conceal it—but, looking back now, what struck her most was how tolerant the famous tenor had been of her openly besotted devotion. Oh, she probably hadn't been the only smitten female student, but she'd always remembered that he'd been kind, and tactful, and had never made her feel juvenile or idiotic.

She would do likewise now, with Philip. His crush, she knew perfectly well, would not outlast the summer. It was only the result of his isolation here, with nothing to do but write his vacation essays...and yearn after her hopelessly, gazing at her ardently with his dark eyes.

Out of nowhere a different image sprang into her head. The man who had walked into her dressing room, invaded her space, had rested his eyes on her—but not with youthful ardour in them. With something far more powerful, more primitive. Long-lashed, heavy-lidded, they had held her in their beam as if she were being targeted by a searchlight. She felt a sudden shimmer go through her—a shiver of sensual awareness—as if she could not escape that focussed regard. Did not want to...

She hauled her mind away.

I don't want to think about it. I don't want to think about him. He asked me out, I said no—that's it. Over and done with.

And it hadn't even been *her* he'd asked out, she reminded herself. The man had taken her for Sabine, sultry and seductive, sophisticated and sexy. She would have to be terminally stupid not to know how a man like that, who thought nothing of approaching a woman he didn't know and asking her to dinner, would have wanted the evening to end had 'Sabine' accepted his invitation. It had been in his eyes, in his gaze—in the way it had washed over her. Blatant in its message.

Would I have wanted it to end that way? If I were Sabine...?

The question was there before she could stop it. Forcibly she pushed it aside, refusing to answer. She was *not* Sabine—she was Sarah Fareham. And whatever the disturbing impact that man had had on her she had no time to dwell on it. She was only weeks away from the most critical performance of her life, and all her energies, all her focus and strength, had to go into that. Nothing else mattered—*nothing*.

'So,' she said, making her voice cheerful, accepting the coffee Philip had poured for her, 'you're our one-man audience, Philip—how's it going, do you think?'

His face lit. 'You were *wonderful*!' he said, his eyes warm upon her.

Damn, thought Sarah wryly, she'd walked into that one. 'Thank you, kind sir,' she said playfully, 'but what about everyone else?'

'I'm sure they're excellent,' said Philip, his lack of interest in the other performers a distinct contrast with his enthusiasm for the object of his devotion. Then he frowned. 'Max treats you very badly,' he said, 'criticising you the way he does.'

Sarah smiled, amused. 'Oh, Philip—that's his job. And it's not just me—he's got to make sure we all get it right and then pull it together. He hears *all* the voices— each of us is focussing only on our own.'

'But yours is *wonderful*,' Philip said, as though that clinched the argument.

She gave a laugh, not answering, and drank her coffee, chasing it down with a large glass of water to freshen her vocal cords.

She was determined to banish the last remnants from the previous night's unwanted encounter with a male who was the very antithesis of the one sitting gazing at her now. Philip's company eased some of the inevitable tension that came from the intensity of rehearsals, the pressure on them all and Max's exacting musical direction. Apart from making sure she did not inadvertently encourage Philip in his crush on her, sitting with him was very undemanding.

With his good-natured, sunny personality, as well as his eagerness and enthusiasm for what was, to him, the novelty of a bohemian, artistic enterprise, it wasn't surprising that she and the other cast members liked him. What had been more surprising to her was that Max had not objected to his presence. His explanation had not found favour with her.

'*Cherie*, anyone staying at their family villa on the *Cap* is loaded. The boy might not throw money around but, believe me, I've checked out the name—he's one rich kid!' Max's eyes had gone to Sarah. 'Cultivate him, *cherie*—we could do with a wealthy sponsor.'

Sarah's reply had been instant—and sharp. 'Don't even *think* of trying to get a donation from him, Max!' she'd warned.

It would be absolutely out of the question for her to take advantage of her young admirer's boyish infatuation, however much family money there might be in the background. She'd pondered whether to warn Philip that Max might be angling for some financial help for the cash-strapped ensemble, but then decided not to. Knowing Philip, it would probably only inspire him to offer it.

She gave a silent sigh. What with treading around Philip's sensibilities, putting her heart and soul into perfecting her performance under the scathing scrutiny of Max, and enduring her nightly ordeal as Sabine, there was a lot on her plate right now. The last thing she needed to be added to it was having her mind straining back with unwelcome insistence to that unnerving visitation to her dressing room the night before.

At her side, Philip was glancing at his watch. He made a face.

'Need to go back to your essays?' she asked sympathetically.

'No,' he answered, 'it's my cousin—the one who owns the villa on the *Cap*—he's turned up on the Riviera and is coming over for lunch.'

'Checking you aren't throwing wild all-night parties, is he?' Sarah teased gently, although Philip was the last type to do any such thing. 'Or holding one himself?'

Philip shook his head. 'Bastiaan's loads too old for that stuff—he's gone thirty,' he said ingenuously. 'He spends most of his time working. Oh, and having hordes of females trailing around after him.'

Well, thought Sarah privately, if Cousin Bastiaan was from the same uber-affluent background as Philip, that wouldn't be too surprising. Rich men, she supposed, never ran short of female attention.

Before she could stop it, her mind homed back to that incident in her dressing room the night before. Her eyes darkened. Now, *there* was a man who was not shy of flaunting his wealth. Dropping invitations to flash restaurants and assuming they'd be snapped up.

But immediately she refuted her own accusation.

He didn't need money to have the impact he had on me. All he had to do was stand there and look at me...

She dragged her mind away. She had to stop this—she *had* to. How many times did she have to tell herself that?

'Sarah!' Max's imperious call rescued her from her troubling thoughts.

She got to her feet, and Philip did too. 'Back to the grindstone,' she said. 'And you scoot, Philip. Have fun with your cousin.' She smiled, lifting a brief hand in farewell as she made her way back to the stage.

Within minutes she was utterly absorbed, her whole being focussed only on her work, and the rest of the world disappeared from sight.

'So,' said Bastiaan, keeping his voice studiedly casual, 'you want to start drawing on your fund, is that it?'

The two of them were sitting outside on the shaded terrace outside the villa's dining room. They'd eaten lunch out there and now Bastiaan was drinking coffee, relaxed back in his chair.

Or rather he appeared to be relaxed. Internally, however, he was on high alert. His young cousin had just raised the subject of his approaching birthday, and asked whether Bastiaan would start to relax the reins now. Warning bells were sounding.

Across the table from him, Philip shifted position. 'It's not going to be a problem, is it?' he said.

He spoke with insouciance, but Bastiaan wasn't fooled. His level of alertness increased. Philip was being evasive.

'It depends.' He kept his voice casual. 'What is it you want to spend the money on?'

Philip glanced away, out over the gardens towards the swimming pool. He fiddled with his coffee spoon some more, then looked back at Bastiaan. 'Is it such a big deal, knowing what I want the money for? I mean, it's *my* money…'

'Yes,' allowed Bastiaan. 'But until your birthday I… I *guard* it for you.'

Philip frowned. 'For me or *from* me?' he said.

There was a tightness in his voice that was new to Bastiaan. Almost a challenge. His level of alertness went up yet another notch.

'It might be the same thing,' he said. His voice was even drier now. Deliberately he took a mouthful of black coffee, replaced the cup with a click on its saucer and looked straight at Philip. 'A fool and his money…' He trailed off deliberately.

He saw his cousin's colour heighten. 'I'm not a fool!' he riposted.

'No,' agreed Bastiaan, 'you're not. But—' he held up his hand '—you could, all the same, be made a fool *of.*'

His dark eyes rested on his cousin. Into his head sprang the image of that *chanteuse* in the nightclub again—pooled in light, her dress clinging, outlining her body like a second skin, her tones low and husky…*alluring…*

He snapped his mind away, using more effort than he was happy about. Got his focus back on Philip—not on the siren who was endangering him. As for his tentative attempt to start accessing his trust fund—well, he'd made his point, and now it was time to lighten up.

'So just remember…' he let humour into his voice now '…when you turn twenty-one you're going to find yourself very, *very* popular—cash registers will start ringing all around you.'

He saw Philip swallow.

'I do know that…' he said.

He didn't say it defiantly, and Bastiaan was glad.

'I really won't be a total idiot, Bast—and…and I'm not ungrateful for your warning. I know—' Bastiaan could hear there was a crack in his voice. 'I know you're keeping an eye on me because…well, because…'

'Because it's what your father would have expected—and what your mother wants,' Bastiaan put in. The humour was gone now. He spoke with only sober sympathy for his grieving cousin and his aunt. He paused. 'She worries about you—you're her only son.'

Philip gave a sad smile. 'Yes, I know,' he said. 'But Bast, please—do reassure her that she truly doesn't need to worry so much.'

'I'll do that if I can,' Bastiaan said. Then, wanting to change the subject completely, he said, 'So, where do you fancy for dinner tonight?'

As he spoke he thought of Le Tombleur. Thought of the rejection he'd had the night before. Unconsciously, his face tightened. Then, as Philip answered, it tightened even more.

'Oh, Bast—I'm sorry—I can't. Not tonight.'

Bastiaan allowed himself a glance. Then, 'Hot date?' he enquired casually.

Colour ran along his cousin's cheekbones. 'Sort of…' he said.

'Sort of hot? Or sort of a date?' Bastiaan kept his probing light. But his mood was not light at all. He'd wondered last night at the club, when he'd checked out the *chanteuse* himself, whether he might see Philip there as well. But there'd been no sign of him and he'd been relieved. Maybe things weren't as bad as he feared. But now—

'A sort of date,' Philip confessed.

Bastiaan backed off. He was walking through landmines for the time being, and he did not want to set one

off. He would have to tread carefully, he knew, or risk
putting the boy's back up and alienating him.

In a burst, Philip spoke again. 'Bast—could I…?
Could you…? Well, there's someone I want you to meet.'

Bastiaan stilled. 'The hot date?' he ventured.

Again the colour flared across his cousin's cheeks.
'Will you?' he asked.

'Of course,' Bastiaan replied easily. 'How would you
like us to meet up? Would you like to invite her to dinner at the villa?'

It was a deliberate trail, and it got the answer he knew
Philip had to give. 'Er…no. Um, there's a place in Les
Pins—the food's not bad—though it's not up to your stan-
dards of course, but—'

'No problem,' said Bastiaan, wanting only to be ac-
commodating. Philip, little did he realise it, was playing
right into his hands. Seeing his cousin with his *inamo-
rata* would give him a pretty good indication of just how
deep he was sunk into the quicksand that she represented.

'Great!'

Philip beamed, and the happiness and relief in his
voice showed Bastiaan that his impressionable, vulnerable cousin was already in way, way too deep…

CHAPTER FOUR

BEYOND THE SPOTLIGHT trained on her, Sarah could see Philip, sitting at the table closest to the stage, gazing up at her while she warbled through her uninspiring medley. At the end of her first set Max went backstage to phone Anton, as he always did, and Sarah stepped carefully down to the dining area, taking the seat Philip was holding out for her.

She smiled across at him. 'I thought you'd be out with your cousin tonight, painting the Côte d'Azur red!' she exclaimed lightly.

'Oh, no,' said Philip dismissively. 'But speaking of my cousin…' He paused, then went on in a rush, 'Sarah, I hope you don't mind… I've asked him here to meet you! You *don't* mind, do you?' he asked entreatingly.

Dismay filled her. She didn't want to crush him, but at the same time the fewer people who knew she appeared here nightly as Sabine the better. Unless, of course, they didn't know her as Sarah the opera singer in the first place.

Philip was a nice lad—a student—but Cousin Bastiaan, for all Sarah knew, moved in the elite, elevated social circles of the very wealthy, and might well be acquainted with any number of people influential in all sorts of areas…including opera. She just could not afford to jeopardise what nascent reputation the festival might build for her—not with her entire future resting on it.

She thought rapidly. 'Look, Philip, I know this might sound confusing, but can we stick to me being Sabine, rather than mentioning my opera singing?' she ventured. 'Otherwise it gets…complicated.'

Complicated was one word for it—*risky* was another.

Philip was looking disconcerted. 'Must I?' he protested. 'I'd love Bastiaan to know how wonderful and talented you really are.' Admiration and ardent devotion shone in his eyes.

Sarah gave a wry laugh. 'Oh, Philip, that's very sweet of you, but—'

She got no further. Philip's gaze had suddenly flicked past her. 'That's him,' he announced. 'Just coming over now—'

Sarah craned her neck slightly—and froze.

The tall figure threading its way towards their table was familiar. Unmistakably so.

She just had time to ask a mental, *What on earth?* when he was upon them.

Philip had jumped to his feet.

'Bast! You made it! Great!' he cried happily, sticking to the French he spoke with Sarah. He hugged his cousin exuberantly, and went on in Greek, 'You've timed it perfectly—'

'Have I?' answered Bastiaan. He kept his voice studiedly neutral, but his eyes had gone to the woman seated at his cousin's table. Multiple thoughts crowded in his head, struggling for predominance. But the one that won out was the last one he wanted.

A jolt of insistent, unmistakable male response to the image she presented.

The twenty-four hours since he'd accosted her in her

dressing room had done nothing at all to lessen the impact she made on him. The same lush blond hair, deep eyes, rich mouth, and another gown that skimmed her shoulders and breasts, moulding the latter to perfection...

He felt his body growl with raw, masculine satisfaction. The next moment he'd crushed it down. So here she was, the sultry *chanteuse*, making herself at home with Philip, and Philip's eyes on her were like an adoring puppy's.

'Bastiaan, I want to introduce you to someone very special,' Philip was saying. A slight flush mounted in the young man's cheeks and his glance went from his cousin to Sarah and back again. 'This...' there was the slightest hesitation in his voice '...this is Sabine.' He paused more discernibly this time. 'Sabine,' he said self-consciously, 'this is my cousin Bastiaan—Bastiaan Karavalas.'

Through the mesh of consternation in Sarah's head one realisation was clear. It was time to call it, she knew. Make it clear to Philip—and to his cousin Bastiaan— that, actually, they were already 'acquainted.' She gave the word a deliberately biting sardonic inflection in her head.

Her long fake lashes dipped down over her eyes and she found herself surreptitiously glancing at the dark-eyed, powerfully built man who had just sat down, dominating the space.

Dominating her senses...

Just as he had the night before, when he'd appeared in her dressing room.

But it wasn't this that concerned her. It was the way he seemed to be suddenly the only person in the entire universe, drawing her eyes to him as irretrievably as if he were the iron to her magnetic compass. She couldn't look away—could only let her veiled glance fasten on him, feel again, as powerfully as she first had, the raw impact he had on her, that sense of power and attraction that she could not explain—did not want to explain.

Call it. She heard the imperative in her head. *Call it—say that you know him—that he has already sought you out...*

But she couldn't do anything other than sit there and try to conjure up some explanation for why she couldn't open her mouth.

Into her head tumbled the overriding question—*What the hell is going on here?*

Because something was—that was for sure. A man she'd never seen before in her life had turned up at the club, bribed a waiter to invite her to his table, then confronted her in her dressing room to ask her out... And then he reappeared as Philip's cousin, unexpectedly arrived in France...

But there was no time to think—no time for anything other than to realise that she had to cope with the situation as it was now and come up with answers later.

'*Mademoiselle...*'

The deep voice was as dark as she remembered it—accented in Greek, similar to Philip's. But that was the only similarity. Philip's voice was light, youthful, his tone usually admiring, often hesitant. But his cousin, in a single word, conveyed to Sarah a whole lot more.

Assessing—guarded—sardonic. Not quite mocking but...

She felt a shiver go down her spine. A shiver she should not be feeling. Should have no need of feeling. Was he *daring* her to admit they'd already encountered one another?

'*M'sieu...*' She kept her voice cool. Totally neutral.

A waiter glided up, seeing a new guest had arrived.

The business of Bastiaan Karavalas ordering a drink—
a dry martini, Sarah noted absently—gave her precious
time to try and grab some composure back.

She was in urgent need of it—whatever Bastiaan Karavalas was playing at, it was his physical presence that
was dominating her senses, overwhelming her with his
raw, physical impact just the way it had last night in her
dressing room. Dragging her gaze to him set her heart
quickening, her pulse surging. What *was* it about him?
That sense of presence, of power—of dark, magnetic attraction? The veiled eyes, the sensual mouth…?

Never had she been so aware of a man. Never had her
body reacted like this.

'For you, *mademoiselle*?' the deep, accented voice
was addressing her, clearly enquiring what she would
like to drink.

She gave a quick shake of her head. 'Thank you—no.
I stick to water between sets.'

He dismissed the waiter with an absent lift of his hand
and the man scurried off to do his bidding.

'Sets?' Bastiaan enquired.

His thoughts were busy. He'd wanted to see whether
she would disclose his approach to her the previous evening, and now he was assessing the implications of her
not doing so.

He was, he knew, assessing a great deal about her…
Predominantly her physical impact on him. Even though
that was the thing least relevant to the situation.

Or was it?

The thought was in his head before he could stop it.
So, too, was the one that followed hard upon its heels.

Her reaction to him blazed from her like a beacon.
Satisfaction—stabbing through him—seared in his veins.
That, oh, *that*, indeed, was something he could use…

He quelled the thought—this was not the time. She had taken the first trick at that first encounter, turning down the invitation he'd so expected her to take. *But the game, Mademoiselle Sabine, is only just begun...*

And he would be holding the winning hand!

'Sa...Sabine's a singer,' Philip was saying, his eyes alight and sweeping admiringly over the *chanteuse* who had him in her coils.

Bastiaan sat back, his eyes flickering over the slinkily dressed and highly made-up figure next to his cousin. 'Indeed?'

It was his turn to use the French language to his advantage—allowing the ironic inflection to work to her discomfiture...as though he doubted the veracity of his cousin's claim.

'Indeed, *m'sieu*,' echoed Sarah. The ironic inflection had not been lost on her and she repaid it herself, in a light, indifferent tone.

He didn't like that, she could see. There was something about the way his dark brows drew a fraction closer to each other, the way the sensual mouth tightened minutely.

'And what do you...sing?' he retaliated, and one dark brow lifted with slight interrogation.

'Chansons d'amour,' Sarah murmured. 'What else?' She gave a smile—just a little one. Light and mocking.

Philip spoke again. 'You've just missed Sabine's first set,' he told Bastiaan.

His glance went to her, as if for reassurance—or perhaps, thought Bastiaan, it was simply because the boy couldn't take his eyes from the woman.

And nor can I—

'But you'll catch her second set!' Philip exclaimed enthusiastically.

'I wouldn't miss it for the world,' he said dryly. Again, his gaze slid to the *chanteuse*.

A new reaction was visible, and it caught his attention. Was he mistaken, or was there, somewhere beneath the make-up, colour suffusing her cheekbones?

Had she taken what he'd said as sarcasm?

If she had, she repaid him in the same coin.

'You are too kind, *m'sieu*,' she said.

And Bastiaan could see, even in the dim light, how her deep-set eyes, so ludicrously enhanced by false eyelashes and heavy kohled lids, flashed fleetingly to green.

A little jolt of sexual electricity fired in him. He wanted to see more of that green flash…

It would come if I kissed her—

'Sa…Sabine's voice is wonderful.'

Philip cut across his heated thoughts. Absently, Bastiaan found himself wondering why his cousin seemed to stammer over the singer's name.

'Even when she's only singing *chan*—'

Sarah's voice cut across Philip's. 'So, M'sieu Karavalas, you have come to visit Philip? I believe the villa is yours, is it not?'

She couldn't care less what he was doing here, or whether he owned a villa on Cap Pierre or anywhere else. She'd only spoken to stop Philip saying something she could see he was dying to say, despite her earlier plea to him—

Even when she's only singing chansons *in a place like this.*

I don't want him to mention anything about what I really sing—that I'm not really Sabine!

Urgency filled her. And now it had nothing to do with not wanting Bastiaan Karavalas to know that Sarah Fareham moonlighted as Sabine Sablon. No, it was for a quite different reason—one that right now seemed far more crucial.

I can't handle him as Sarah. I need to be Sabine. Sabine can cope with this—Sabine can cope with a man like him. Sabine is the kind of sophisticated, worldly-wise female who can deal with such a man.

With the kind of man who coolly hit on a woman who'd taken his eye and aroused his sexual interest, arrogantly assuming she would comply without demur. The kind of man who rested assessing, heavy-lidded eyes on her, drawing no veil over what he saw in her, knowing exactly what impact his assessment of her was having.

That kind of man...

Philip's enthusiastic voice was a relief to her.

'You ought to spend some time at the villa, Bast! It really is a beautiful place. Paulette says you're hardly ever there.'

Bastiaan flicked his eyes to his cousin. 'Well, maybe I should move across from Monaco and stay awhile with you. Keep you on the straight and narrow.'

He smiled at Philip, and as he did so Sarah suddenly saw a revelation. Utterly unexpected. Gone—totally vanished—was the Bastiaan Karavalas she'd been exposed to, with his coolly assessing regard and his blatant appraisal, and the sense of leashed power that emanated from him. Now, as he looked across at Philip, his smile carved deep lines around his mouth and lightened his expression, made him suddenly seem... different.

She felt something change inside her—uncoil as if a knot had been loosened...

If he ever smiled at me like that I would be putty in his hands.

But she sheered her mind away. Bastiaan Karavalas

was unsettling enough, without throwing such a smile her way.

'Make me write all my wretched essays, you mean—don't you, Bast?' Philip answered, making a face.

But Sarah could see the communication running between them, the easy affection. It seemed to make Bastiaan far less formidable. But that, she knew with a clenching of her muscles, had a power of its own. A power she must not acknowledge. Not even as Sabine.

'It's what you came here for,' Bastiaan reminded him. 'And to escape, of course.'

His dark eyes flickered back to Sarah and the warmth she'd seen so fleetingly as he'd smiled at his young cousin drained out of them. It was replaced by something new. Something that made her eyes narrow minutely as she tried to work out what it was.

'I offered the villa to Philip as a refuge,' he informed Sarah in a casual voice. 'He was being plagued by a particularly persistent female. She made a real nuisance of herself, didn't she?' His glance went back to his cousin.

Philip made another face. 'Elena Constantis *was* a pain,' he said feelingly. 'Honestly, she's got boys buzzing all over her, but she still wanted to add *me* to her stupid collection. She's so immature,' he finished loftily.

A tiny smile hovered at Sarah's lips, dispelling her momentary unease. Immaturity was a relative term, after all. For a second—the briefest second—she caught a similar smile just tugging at Bastiaan Karavalas's well-shaped mouth, lifting it the way his smile at Philip had done a moment ago.

Almost, *almost* she felt herself starting to meet his eyes, ready to exchange glances with him—two people so much more mature than sweet, young Philip...

Then the intention was wiped from her consciousness.

Its tempting potency gone. Philip's gaze had gone to her. 'She couldn't be more different from *you*,' he said. The warmth in his voice could have lit a fire.

Sarah's long, fake eyelashes dipped again. Bastiaan Karavalas's dark gaze had switched to her, and she was conscious of it—burningly conscious of it. Conscious, too, of what must have accounted for the studiedly casual remark he'd made that had got them on to this subject.

Surely he can't think I don't realise that Philip is smitten with me?

Bastiaan was speaking again. 'Sabine is certainly much *older*,' he observed.

The dark eyes had flicked back to her face—watching, she could tell, for her reaction to his blunt remark. Had he intended to warn her? To show her how real his cousin's infatuation with her was?

How best to respond…? 'Oh, I'm ancient, indeed!' she riposted lightly. 'Positively creaking.'

'You're not old!' Philip objected immediately, aghast at the very idea. Adoration shone in his eyes. Then his gaze shifted to the dance floor in front of the stage, where couples had started to congregate. His face lit. 'Oh! Sabine—will you dance with me? Please say yes!'

Indecision filled her. She never danced with Philip or did anything to encourage him. But right now it would get her away from the disturbing, overpowering impact of Bastiaan Karavalas.

'If you like,' she replied, and got to her feet as he leapt eagerly to his and walked her happily out on to the dance floor.

Thankfully, the music was neither very fast—fast dancing would have been impossible in her tight gown—nor so slow that it would require any kind of smoochy embrace. But since most of the couples were in a traditional ballroom-style hold with each other, that was the hold she glided into.

Philip, bless him, clearly wasn't too *au fait* with so formal a dancing style, but he manfully did his best. 'I've got two left feet!' he exclaimed ruefully.

'You're doing fine,' she answered encouragingly, making sure she was holding him literally at arm's length.

It seemed an age until the number finally ended.

'Well done,' she said lightly.

'I won't be so clumsy next time,' he promised her.

She let her hand fall from his shoulder and indicated that he should let go of her too—which he did, with clear reluctance. But Philip's crush on her was not uppermost in her mind right now.

She was just about to murmur something about her next set, and this time make sure she headed off, when a deep voice sounded close by.

'Mademoiselle Sabine? I trust you will give me equal pleasure?'

She started, her head twisting. Bastiaan Karavalas was bearing down on them as the music moved on to another number. A distinctly slower number.

He gave her no chance to refuse. An amused nod of dismissal at his cousin and then, before she could take the slightest evasive action, Sarah's hand had been taken, her body was drawn towards his by the placing of his large, strong hand at her waist, and she was forced to lift her other hand and let it rest as lightly as she could on his shoulder. Then he was moving her into the dance—his thigh pressing blatantly against hers to impel her to move.

Instinctively Sarah tried to preserve her composure, though her heart was pounding in her ribcage. Her body was as stiff as a board, her muscles straining away from him as if she could increase the narrow gap between their bodies. His answer was to curve his fingers into her waist, and with effortless strength secure his hold on her again.

He smiled down at her.

It was a smile of pure possession.

Sarah could feel her blood surging in her body, quickening in every vein, heating her from within as she moved against his possessive clasp.

'So, *mademoiselle*, on what shall we converse?'

His smile had given way to a question in which both irony and amusement were mingled. And something else too—something she could not give a name to, but which seemed to send yet another quiver of excruciating physical awareness of his closeness to her.

Yet again she found herself clinging to the persona of Sabine. Sabine could cope with this—Sabine could let the potently powerful Bastiaan Karavalas sweep her off and yet keep her cool about it. Keep her composure. So what would Sabine do...say...?

'The choice is yours, *m'sieu*,' she answered, managing to keep her tone somewhere between insouciant and indifferent. Social...civil...just this side of courteous. She made herself meet his gaze, the way Sabine undoubtedly would—for what would Sabine be overset by in those dark, sensual eyes? And Sabine's ridiculously long fake lashes helped, Sarah thought with gratitude, because their length made it easier for her to look at him with a veiled expression—helped her feel protected from the impact those deep, dark eyes were having on her...

Abruptly, he spoke, yanking her back to full focus. 'Why did you not mention that you had already made my acquaintance?' he said.

Sarah felt her eyes widening. There was only one answer to give. 'Why didn't *you*?' she said. She sought to copy the dismissive inflection that Sabine would surely give.

Her answer was a sudden opacity in his gaze. 'You must know why—' he said.

From his dark, deep-set eyes a message blazed that was as clear as day...as old as time.

Sarah could feel her breath catch in her throat, her pulse leap—and suddenly Sabine, with all her worldly defences, felt a long, long way away.

'Why did you refuse to come to dinner with me?' Again, the question was blunt—challenging. Taking her by surprise.

'You were a complete stranger.' She sought for the only explanation that was relevant—whether or not it was one that Sabine would have made.

Thoughts flickered across her mind like random electric currents. Would Sabine have found that objectionable? Or would she have made her decision about whether to let a man take her to dinner—and what might follow—on quite different grounds?

Such as if the man were the most devastating male she'd ever set eyes on—who'd had the most powerful impact on her she'd ever experienced—who'd stilled the breath in her lungs and sent her pulse into overdrive...

But she was given no opportunity to think coherently about that, or about anything at all, because now his eyes had a glint in them that was setting her pulse racing even faster.

'Well, I am not a stranger now.'

Not when I hold you in the intimacy of this embrace... your soft, satiny body in my arms, the warmth of your palm against mine, the brush of your thighs as we move to the music together...

He felt the flush of heat beating in his veins. Telling him how susceptible he was to what she possessed.

The power to make him desire her...

His senses were overpowering him. There was a lingering perfume about her—not cloying, as he might have expected, but faintly floral. Her hair, curved around her shoulder as it was, was not sticky with spray but fine and silky. He wanted to feel it running through his fingers. Wanted to drink in the fine-boned beauty of her face, see again that flash of emeralds in her eyes...

A sudden impulse possessed him. To wipe her complexion free of the mask of make-up covering it and see her true beauty revealed.

'Why do you wear so much make-up?' His question came from nowhere—he hadn't meant to ask it.

She looked momentarily startled. 'It's stage make-up,' she answered. She spoke as if she found it hard to believe he'd asked.

He frowned. 'It does not flatter you,' he stated.

Now, *why* had he said that? he grilled himself. Why tell this woman such a thing?

Because it is the truth—she masks her true beauty, her true self, behind such excess.

Her expression changed. 'It's not designed to flatter—only to withstand the stage lighting. You don't imagine that I wear these spiders on my eyes for any other reason, do you?' Her voice was dry.

'Good,' he said, giving a brief nod.

Even as he did so he realised he was way off agenda. What on earth was he *doing*, talking about her stage make-up? Let alone expressing approval—relief?—that it *was* only make-up. He sought to resume the line of enquiry he'd started. That was the reason he was dancing with her—so that he could continue his assessment of her. Purely for the purposes for which he'd arrived in France, of course…

To free his cousin from her.

Free her from Philip—

The thought was there—indelible, inadmissible. He wiped it instantly. There was no question of freeing *her* from his cousin. It was Philip—only Philip—he was concerned about. That was what he had to remember.

Not the way her body was moving with his to the soft, seductive cadences of the music, drawing them closer and closer to each other…

Not the way her fragrance was coiling into his senses. Not the way his eyes were lingering on her face…her parted lips… The way he was feeling the soft breath coming from her…intoxicating him…

The melody ended. He stopped abruptly. Even more abruptly she disengaged herself from his grasp. But she did not move—simply stood there for a moment, continuing to gaze at him. As if she could not stop…

Her breasts, Bastiaan could see, were rising and falling as if her breathing were rapid—her pulse was more rapid still. Colour was in her cheeks, beneath the thick layer of foundation. He could just see it…sense it…

Her gaze was dragged from him, back across to where Philip was sitting, his expression a mixture of impatience at her absence, discontent that she had been dancing with his cousin, and his usual fixed regard of uncritical admiration.

She walked across to him—her dress felt tighter suddenly, and she was all too conscious of the swaying movement of her hips. She could almost *feel* Bastiaan Karavalas watching her…

She reached the table. Philip stood up immediately, his chair scraping.

'Phew!' she said, pointedly not resuming her seat. 'I'm worn out by dancing. Two dances and two partners—quite an evening for me!' She spoke with deliberate lightness, obvious humour. Reaching for her glass of water, she took a quick gulp, finding she needed it, then set it down. 'I must go backstage,' she said. 'Prep for my next set.'

Conscious that Philip's cousin was standing behind her, she could say very little else to Philip. She took a step away, encompassing Bastiaan Karavalas in her movement.

'I'll bid you goodnight,' she said, making her voice sound nothing more than effortlessly casual.

She had to get control back—the way Sabine would. Sabine would have been utterly unfazed by that slow, seductive dance with Bastiaan Karavalas. Sabine wouldn't have felt as if her whole body were trembling, her senses overwhelmed. No, Sabine would stay composed, unruffled—would be well used to men like Bastiaan Karavalas desiring her.

Philip was speaking and she made herself pay attention, drag her thoughts away from his cousin.

'I'll see you tomorrow at the…here…?' he asked.

Sarah was relieved that he'd just avoided saying *at the rehearsal*.

She smiled. A warm smile. Because she didn't want to hurt him, and his feelings were so transparent. 'Why not?' she said lightly. 'Unless…' And now her eyes found Bastiaan again. 'Unless you and your cousin have plans…? You must make the most of him while he's here.'

Dark lashes flickered over even darker eyes. She saw it—caught it. 'I may well be here some time,' Bastiaan Karavalas said. 'It all depends…'

She made no answer—could only give a vague, brief

smile and bestow a little wave on Philip, because she wanted to be nice to him, and he was so young, and felt so much...

And then she was gone, whisking away through a little door inset into the wall beside the low stage.

Slowly, Bastiaan sat down. Philip did too, but Bastiaan said nothing—his head was full. Far too full. Only one thought was predominant—he wanted to hear her sing... he wanted to feast his eyes on her again.

Feast so much more than his eyes...

CHAPTER FIVE

As SARAH TOOK her place on the stage she was burningly aware of those dark, heavy eyes upon her. It was the same sensation she'd had the previous night, when she hadn't known who was watching her—had only been able to feel it. As she felt it now, again, that same sense of exposure. But now there was so much more—now there was a frisson running through her body, her veins, that came from his heavy-lidded perusal.

Why? The question kept circling in her head. Why was she reacting like this? Why was this man—this dark, disturbing cousin of Philip—able to arouse such a response in her? Never, *never* before had she been so affected by a man.

By a man's desire for her.

Because it is a desire that echoes in me too...

That was the truth of it. Out of nowhere, like a bolt of lightning crashing into tinder-dry trees, he'd set her alight....

A sense almost of panic swept over her.

I can't handle it. I'm not used to it. No man has ever made me feel this way—like I'm on fire, burning from the inside. I don't know what to do—how to react...

Nothing with Andrew had prepared her for this. Nothing!

I didn't know it was possible to feel this way. To feel this overwhelmed—this helpless.

This aroused...

Standing there in the spotlight, knowing that the dark, heavy eyes of Bastiaan Karavalas were resting on her, that she was exposed to his view, her body had reacted as if her flesh were aflame.

She wanted to run, bolt from the stage, but that was impossible. Impossible to do anything but continue to stand there, the microphone between her fingers, her voice intimate.

While Bastiaan Karavalas looked his fill of her.

No! The cry came from within. *It isn't me he's gazing at—it's Sabine. Sabine is standing here, feeling like this.*

And Sabine—Sabine could handle it. Of course she could. Sabine was not helpless or overwhelmed by the blatant desire in those dark, heavy eyes.

Or by her own desire...

Sabine was who she must be to cope with what was happening to her, with the fire that was running in her veins, burning her senses. That was what she clung to as she worked her way through her numbers.

Never had her set seemed longer, and how she got through it she wasn't sure, but in the end she was heading off stage, filled with relief.

As she gained her dressing room she saw Philip waiting. He launched in as soon as he could.

'Sarah—this Sunday—will you...will you come over to the villa for lunch?' He got the words out in a rush, his eyes filled with eager hope. 'I've been wanting to ask you, but it was Bast who suggested it.'

She felt a quiver inside her, even though she strove to stanch it. *Why? Why had Bastiaan Karavalas suggested inviting her to his villa?*

And the only answer she could think of sent that quiver vibrating through her again, quickening her pulse.

I don't have time for this. I don't have time to have Bastiaan Karavalas looking at me the way he does, have the impact on me he does. I just don't have time—not now. And I can't cope with it anyway—can't cope with him. I don't know how to respond or react. And, anyway, it isn't me he's inviting—it's Sabine! Sabine's the one he's drawn to—not me. He wants what Sabine would offer him...

The hectic thoughts tumbled through her mind, incoherent and confused. She had to answer somehow—but what? And how?

'So, will you come? Please say yes,' Philip's eager voice pressed.

She pulled herself together forcibly. 'I'm…I'm not sure…' she got out.

'What's this you're plotting?'

Max's voice sounded behind her. It sounded amused, but with a pointedness in it that Sarah was not deaf to.

Philip turned. 'I was asking Sarah if she would come over to the villa for lunch on Sunday with my cousin and me,' he relayed.

'Cousin?' Max raised his eyebrows.

'My cousin—Bastiaan Karavalas,' supplied Philip. 'It's his villa I'm staying at. He's visiting me from Greece.'

'Karavalas…' murmured Max.

Sarah knew he was storing the information away and would check it out later—just as he'd checked out Philip's name. Any cousin of Philip's would be rich as well, and for that reason she knew she might be disheartened by what Max said next, but she could not be surprised.

Max smiled at Philip. 'Why wait till Sunday?' he said

blandly. 'Make it tomorrow—I'll rejig the schedule so Sarah can get away at noon. How would that be?'

Philip's face lit. 'Fantastic! I'll go and tell Bast now. Brilliant!'

He beamed at Sarah and Max, and then rushed off to front of house.

Sarah turned to Max. 'Max—' she began, about to remonstrate.

Max held up a hand. 'Say nothing. I know your opinion about asking Philip for money. But...' his voice changed 'But this Bastiaan Karavalas, the cousin—well, that's a different matter, isn't it? A grown man who owns a villa on Cap Pierre—and presumably a whole lot else— doesn't require kid-glove-handling, does he? So, *cherie*, off you go to lunch with these lovely rich people and make yourself agreeable to them.'

Sarah's expression hardened. 'Max, if you think—'

'*Cherie*, it's just lunch—nothing more than that. What did you *think* I was suggesting?'

He sounded amused, and it irritated Sarah. 'I don't know and I don't care,' she shot back, shutting her dressing room door in his face.

Consternation was flooding through her. She did not *want* to go over to Bastiaan Karvalas's villa and spend the afternoon there. She didn't want to spend a single moment more in his company. Didn't want another opportunity for him to work his dark, potent magic on her senses...

I don't need this distraction. I have to focus on the festival—it's all that's important to me. Nothing else. I want Bastiaan Karavalas gone—out of my life!

She stilled suddenly as she started to change out of her costume. Her mind raced.

Maybe going to the villa wasn't so bad an idea after

all. Maybe she could turn the invitation to her advantage. Find an opportunity to get Bastiaan Karavalas on his own and suggest that it would be a really good idea for him to whisk Philip away. Distance would soon cause his youthful crush to atrophy.

And it would take Bastiaan Karavalas away as well… Stop him disturbing her the way he did so that she could get back to the only important thing in her life now: preparing for the festival. Not being swept away by what was in his dark, desiring eyes.

Yes. She took a steadying breath. That, surely, would make it worth enduring an afternoon of his company. Because there was no other reason for wanting to spend an afternoon with Bastiaan Karavalas.

Liar, said a voice inside her head. A voice that whispered to her in Sabine's soft, seductive tones…

'She'll come over tomorrow!' Philip exclaimed happily as he re-joined Bastiaan.

'How surprising…' murmured Bastiaan.

Of course Mademoiselle Sabine had jumped at the invitation to get a foot…literally…in the door.

His cousin completely missed the sardonic note in his voice. 'Isn't it?' he answered. 'Considering how—' he stopped short.

Bastiaan cocked an eyebrow. 'Considering…?' he prompted.

'Oh, nothing,' Philip answered hastily, but looked as if he were hiding something.

Yet again the question fired in Bastiaan's head. *How far has this infatuation gone? What is Philip hiding?*

But surely his instincts were correct? Philip was not radiating the aura of a young man who had achieved possession of the object of his desire and devotion. He was still worshipping at the altar.

A silent growl of raw, male satisfaction rasped through him. Its occurrence did not please him. Just the opposite. Damnation—the very thought that he could be *glad* that Philip was still merely mooning over the delectable blonde singer for any other reason than that it meant that it would be easier separating him from Sabine, extricating him from her toils, was unacceptable.

He changed the subject deliberately. 'So—tonight... Do you want to come over to Monte? We can eat out and you can stay at my apartment.'

Again, it was a deliberate trail, to discover whether Philip would otherwise have been heading towards La Belle Sabine for a midnight tryst...

To his satisfaction Philip was perfectly amenable to this suggestion, helping Bastiaan to confirm his judgement that, however besotted Philip was with the woman, it had not yet progressed to anything more...tangible.

Then another, more unwelcome thought struck him. *Is she holding out on bestowing herself upon him until he has control over his own funds?*

Was that her game plan? His expression hardened as they left the club. He was looking forward to lunch tomorrow—it would give him more time to study her. Assess her.

All for the sake of rescuing his cousin, of course. Not for any other reason...

None that he would permit.

'Stop!' Max threw his hand up impatiently. 'I said *sostunuto*, not *diminuendo*! If you can't tell the difference, Sarah, believe me—I can! Take it again.'

Sarah drew her breath in sharply but said nothing,

though her jaw was set. Max was being particularly ty-
rannical this morning, and Alain, her tenor, playing The
Soldier, was fractious. So was she, she admitted to herself. She was hitting vocal difficulties all over the place,
and it was frustrating the hell out of her. The rehearsal
session was not going smoothly and Max was finding
fault with all of them. Nerves were getting jittery all
round.

She shut her eyes to center herself.

'In your own time, Sarah,' came Max's sarcastic
prompt.

Somehow her next attempt managed to assuage him,
and he turned his exacting attention to Alain and his apparently many flaws, before resuming his attack on Sarah
for the next passage that displeased him.

By the time he dismissed her Sarah felt ragged. She
definitely needed fresh air and a change of environment.
For the first time she actually felt grateful that she was
to have the afternoon off, courtesy of Philip's invitation.
As she scooped up her bag she heard Max start in on the
alto and the baritone, and hurried to make her escape
from the fraught atmosphere.

Philip had texted to say he'd pick her up from her *pension*, where she headed now to change into something
suitable for having lunch at a millionaire's villa on the
exclusive Cap Pierre.

Just what constituted 'suitable'? she pondered.

In the end there was only one outfit that was possible. It was one she'd bought when she'd first arrived in
France to join the opera company, after the school term
had ended. It wasn't her usual floaty, floral style, but a
chic sixties-style shift in a shade of green that suited her
fair colouring.

She pushed her hair back with a white band, and completed the retro look with pastel lipstick, frosted eyeshadow and a lot of eyeliner.

She studied her reflection—yes, definitely more Sabine than Sarah. Just what she needed.

'Oh, my goodness!' she exclaimed as she stepped outdoors and immediately saw the low, lean, bright red Ferrari parked there.

'Isn't it a beauty?' Philip said lovingly. 'It's Bast's. He keeps it in Monte Carlo—he has an apartment there as well—and he's letting me drive it today.'

He sounded awestruck at the prospect.

'Bast's already at the villa,' Philip explained, helping her into the low, luxurious passenger seat. 'So...' He looked at her expectantly, his eyes alight, as he started the engine with a throaty growl. 'What do you think?'

She gave a laugh. 'Terrifying!' she said feelingly.

He laughed, as though he could not possibly believe her, and moved off. He was obviously thrilled by driving such a powerful, fabulous car, and Sarah wisely let him concentrate. The road leading out on to the *Cap* was a residential one, with a modest speed limit.

It was only five minutes to the villa, and she could see Philip's reluctance to abandon the vehicle when he arrived. It seemed, she thought dryly, and not with regret, that she finally had a rival.

Well, any rival was to be welcomed, even one with wheels. What she really wanted to conjure up, though, was a flesh and blood rival to take his mind off *her*—someone suitable for his age and circumstances. She frowned slightly. What had Bastiaan Karavalas been saying the previous evening? About dispatching Philip to his villa in the first place because he'd been pursued by some spoilt teen in Greece? That was a *good* sign, because it could only mean that Philip's cousin would be amenable to her suggesting that another rescue was needed.

Except that I'm going to have to speak to him alone.

That was *not* something she wanted to have to do. Not even behind the protection of being Sabine. But right now she would grab any protection she could.

Walking into the white-plastered, low-rise villa, set in spacious grounds out on the promontory of the *Cap,* she felt the need of Philip's familiar innocuous presence as they crossed the cool, stone-floored hall into a wide reception room and she saw the tall, sable-haired figure of Bastiaan Karavalas strolling in from the vine-shaded terrace beyond to greet them.

As she had the night before, and the first time she'd laid eyes on him, Sarah felt an instinctive, automatic reaction to him. It was like a switch being thrown inside her—a buzz of electric current in her veins, a kick in her heartbeat. She saw his dark eyes narrow as they lit on her, and the electric current ran again—and then Philip was greeting him and ushering her forward.

'Here we are, Bast,' he said cheerfully. 'Is lunch ready? I'm starving. Are we eating out on the terrace?'

'We've time for a drink first,' Bastiaan replied, and Sarah saw that he was carrying a champagne bottle in one hand and three glasses loosely by their stems in the other. 'But let's head out anyway. *Mademoiselle...?'*

He stepped aside from the door to let her go through first. It meant passing close to him, and she felt his eyes on her as she walked out on to the terrace. Then all thoughts of the disturbing Bastiaan Karavalas left her.

'Oh, this is *beautiful!*' she heard herself exclaim.

The wide, shady terrace, roofed by vines and vivid bougainvillaea, opened to verdant lawns beyond, which were edged with richly foliated bushes and sloped down to a glittering azure pool, behind which stretched the even more glitteringly azure reaches of the Mediterranean Sea.

'Welcome to my villa, Sabine,' said Bastiaan.

She turned at the accented voice. His eyes were sweeping over her and she could feel their impact. Feel the electricity course through her again.

Not in a tuxedo, as she had previously seen him, but in a pair of long, pale grey chinos and a short-sleeved, dark burgundy open-necked polo shirt, which moulded his powerful torso. He looked lean, lithe and devastatingly attractive. She felt her stomach give a little clench of appreciation.

'Sab—come and sit down,' Philip was saying, indicating the ironwork table set for lunch.

He'd taken to calling her 'Sab' on the way there, and Sarah was glad. It might make him less likely to call her Sarah. She was also glad about her choice of outfit. OK, so she was probably slightly too smartly dressed for what was clearly going to be an al fresco meal, with Bastiaan in casual clothes and Philip in his customary designer-labelled T-shirt and jeans, but her retro-chic dress felt almost like a costume—and that *had* to help her be Sabine and not Sarah, who was perilously out of her depth in such deep waters as swirled about this powerfully, devastatingly sensual male...

As she carefully seated herself where Philip was holding a chair out for her, in a position that afforded her a view right out over the gardens, she could feel those heavy-lidded eyes on her while Bastiaan settled himself at the head of the table.

'May I tempt you to champagne, Sabine?' The deep-voiced question required an answer.

'Thank you,' she said politely. Inside, the inner voice

that whispered to her so seductively in Sabine's husky tones was teasing her... *You tempt me to so much more...*

She silenced it sharply, making herself look not at the man who drew her eyes, but instead out over the beautiful gardens to the sea beyond. Her expression softened. It really was absolutely beautiful, she thought with genuine pleasure. Private, verdant, full of flowers, with the azure sea sparkling beyond—a true Mediterranean idyll.

'What a beautiful spot this is!' she could not help exclaiming warmly. 'If it were mine I'd never leave!'

'Oh, Bast has an entire island to himself at home,' Philip answered. 'This place is tiny in comparison.'

Sarah's eyes widened. Bastiaan saw it as he busied himself opening the champagne. *Thank you, Philip*, he thought, *that was helpful*. His appreciation was sincere—he wanted to see how Sabine reacted to his wealth. Whether it would cause her to turn her attentions to him instead of his cousin.

And would that be helpful too? Again he found himself contemplating using that method to detach her from Philip. It might be so much...*swifter*.

Enjoyable...

His eyes rested on her as he filled their glasses. He was still trying to get past his first reaction to her when he'd walked out on to the terrace. It had been—*surprise*.

Oh, he'd known, obviously, that she wouldn't turn up for lunch in a skin-tight evening gown and a face full of stage make-up. But he'd expected her to wear some kind of flashy strapless brief sundress, exposing a lot of thigh and with a slashed décolletage, and to be adorned with jangly gold jewellery, her hair in a tousled mane. But her stylishly retro look had a chicness to it that drew his eye without condemnation.

Interesting, he found himself thinking. She had

changed her image decisively. At the nightclub she had been all sultry vamp. Today she had moved on a couple of decades to the swinging sixties—almost as though she'd made a costume change between acts...

But then, he thought caustically, putting on an act was what a woman like Sabine was all about, wasn't it? From standing on a stage singing throaty, amorous numbers for strangers, to manipulating the emotions of a smitten, impressionable youth.

His eyes hardened minutely as they rested on her. *You will find it harder to manipulate me, mademoiselle...*

If there was any manipulating to be done, then it would be coming from *him*—not her. He would be the one to steer her in the precise direction he wished her to go—away from Philip. *And to me instead?* Again the thought played in his mind provocatively. Temptingly.

'I imagine a private island is just about *de rigueur* for a Greek tycoon, isn't it?' she was saying now, lightly, with a clear infusion of amusement in her voice.

Bastiaan sat back in his chair, lifting his glass. 'Do you take me for a tycoon, *mademoiselle*?' he riposted.

But there was a deep timbre in his voice all the same. She felt it like a low vibration in her body.

'Oh, surely you could be nothing less, *m'sieu*?' she answered in kind. 'With your private island in the Aegean!'

She had matched the slight tinge of ironic inflection that had been in his voice and suddenly there seemed to be a flicker in his dark eyes, a slight curve of his mouth, as if for her alone... Something she didn't want to be there.

Something she did...

No, no I don't. And, anyway, isn't it bad enough that I've got to deal with Philip's bad attack of calf love? The last thing I need is to develop a crush of my own on his cousin.

She paused. Crush? Was *that* what she was calling this strange, disturbing electricity between them? This ridiculous, absurd awareness of his overpowering physical impact on her? A *crush*?

Negation leapt in her. No, this was no crush. There was only one cause for what she was feeling about this man who had walked into her dressing room that night, who had taken her in his powerful, controlling clasp on the dance floor, who was now watching her, his heavy eyes half lidded, waiting for her to reply in similar vein...

Desire. Raw, insistent desire. Desire bred of her burning awareness of his presence, of his physical existence—the way the tough line of his jaw squared his face, the way the strong column of his throat rose from the open neck of his polo, the way the sable darkness of his hair feathered the broad brow, the way his shirt moulded across the strength of his shoulders, his torso...

Desire—that was the only word for it. The only name to give what she was feeling now as her body flushed with heat, with awareness...

Desperation spiked in her. It was like a sideways sweeping wave, knocking her askew, derailing her. And she could not allow it to happen. Not with her whole life's ambition consuming her right now. That was all she must think of—that was all she must focus on.

Not on this man who can make my pulse catch just by letting his dark, dark eyes rest on me, setting my senses afire...

It was a fire she had to quench—and fast.

She reached for her champagne, needing its potency to regain control of herself.

'Bast's island's in the Ionian Sea, not the Aegean,' Philip was saying. 'Off the west coast of Greece. Not far from Zakynthos.'

Sarah turned her head towards him, half reluctant, half grateful to drag her gaze away from his darkly disturbing cousin. 'I don't know Greece at all,' she said. 'I've never been.'

'I'd love to show you. You'd love Athens!' Philip replied immediately, his voice full of enthusiasm.

A low laugh came from the other end of the table. 'A city full of ancient ruins? I doubt it. I'm sure Sabine would prefer sophisticated cities, like Milan or Paris.'

She didn't correct him. The real Sabine, wherever she was right now, probably *would* prefer such cities, and at the moment that persona was hers. She'd better let the issue lie.

She gave a very Gallic shrug, as she had so often seen her French mother give.

'I like warm climates,' she answered, which seemed an unrevealing comment to make, and was true as well. The Yorkshire winters she'd grown up with had never been her favourite, nor her mother's either. She had preferred the soft winters of her native Normandy. She looked at Philip again. 'I couldn't stand the frozen East Coast USA winters you have at uni.'

Philip shivered extravagantly. 'Neither can I!' He laughed. 'But we get snow in Greece sometimes—don't we, Bast?'

'There is even skiing in the mountains,' his cousin agreed.

'Bast skis like a champion!' Philip exclaimed, with open admiration for his older cousin.

'I was at school in Switzerland,' Bastiaan said laconically, by way of explanation.

Sarah's glance went back to Bastiaan. 'Is that why your French is so good?' she asked.

'Oh, Bast's fluent in German as well—aren't you,

Bast? And English, of course. *My* English is probably better than my French, actually, so really we should be speaking—'

'Tell me more about your private island.' Sarah's voice cut across Philip, preventing him from finishing his sentence. She was starting to think that this was ridiculous—all this stuff about her being Sabine. She should just come right out with it—trust Philip's cousin with her real identity and be done with it.

But she was conscious of a deep reluctance to do so. Partly, she knew, for the reason she'd given Philip—but that was not the overwhelming reason. Being Sabine gave her...*protection*. Protection from the onslaught on her senses that Bastiaan Karavalas was making on her.

'My private island?' Bastiaan echoed her. 'What can I tell you? Acreage? Location? Value?'

There was a quizzical expression in his voice, and he spoke lightly, yet Sarah could see a twist at the corner of his mouth. She found herself wondering at it, but her focus had to be on continuing the conversation. She didn't really care that much about Bastiaan Karavalas's island, but it had been the first thing she'd been able to think of asking about in order to interrupt Philip.

'What do you do on it?'

The quizzical expression came again, but this time she had the feeling it was genuine—as if her question had been unexpected. She watched him lift his champagne flute to his mouth.

'Do?' he said. 'Very little.' He gave a sudden smile, taking a mouthful of champagne. 'I take a dinghy out sometimes...swim, chill...not much else. Oh, I read sometimes too—or just watch the sun set with a glass of beer at my side. Nothing exciting. You, *mademoiselle*, would find it very dull.'

Even as he spoke Bastiaan found himself wondering. Why hadn't she followed up on his deliberate mentions of its size and value? Gone on to draw him out about the other properties he owned? Like his villa in the Caribbean, his condo in Manhattan, his apartment in London, his mansion in Athens… It was inconsistent of her. She'd been keen to get him to talk about owning the island in the first place, getting him to reveal to her just how wealthy he actually was.

'*Au contraire,*' she riposted, and Bastiaan became aware of the greenness of her eyes. 'It sounds very relaxing.'

She held his gaze a moment, and into his head sprang the image of just how he might 'relax' with such a woman on his private island… He felt a kick go through him—one that told him her impact on him was as powerful as ever.

Should I respond to it? Respond to the allure she has for me? Use it for my own purpose?

The questions came—but not the answers… And the very fact that the questions were forming in his mind indicated the temptation they presented. Showed him the answers he wanted to give…

His thoughts were interrupted by Paulette, emerging with the lunch tray. Philip got to his feet to take it from her and was rewarded by a beaming smile—clearly his young cousin had become a favourite of the housekeeper. As he and Philip started to unload it, he noticed Sabine was helping as well, passing plates of *charcuterie* and *fromage*, salads and crusty baguette slices.

'Would you like wine, or are you happy to stick to champagne?' Bastiaan enquired of his guest courteously.

Sarah smiled. 'What girl wouldn't be happy to stick to champagne?' she replied humorously.

She was working hard to keep her tone light, inconsequential. After lunch she must find an opportunity to get Bastiaan on his own, to broach to him her recommendation that it might be best to remove his young cousin to another place that offered less distraction. But even as she determined to do it she found herself dreading it. Dreading being on her own with Bastiaan Karavalas for any time at all.

Roughly, she shook such thoughts from herself. Sought to find something innocuous to say... 'Though if I drink too much at lunchtime I may well fall fast asleep in the afternoon.'

Bastiaan laughed, and yet again Sarah felt her pulse quicken. 'You would be quite welcome,' he said, and indicated the sun loungers that were set out on the lawn beneath the shade of a parasol.

'Don't tempt me,' she riposted, reaching for a piece of bread.

But you do *tempt me, Mademoiselle Sabine—you tempt me greatly...*

Again, the words took shape in his head before he could unsay them. Unthink them...

As he started to help himself to lunch Bastiaan could feel thoughts swirling. Would it *really* be so bad to let his interest in Sabine take the direction in which he could feel it drawing him? Had since his first moment of setting eyes on her.

She tempts me—and without a doubt she feels desire for me, answering my desire for her...

He could hear the arguments in his head already—as tempting as this beautiful woman was.

It would achieve the end I seek...the purpose of my journey—it would take her away from Philip, set him free from his infatuation. And give me what I want...

There was so much in its favour. Why should he reject such a solution to the problem?

Through half-veiled eyes he watched as Philip fussed over her, offering her dishes from the table.

'Chicken, brie and grapes would be lovely,' she said.

Her smile on his cousin was warm, and Bastiaan could see Philip drinking it in. Out of nowhere, a needle pricked Bastiaan beneath the skin.

I want her to smile like that at me.

Jerkily, he reached for the champagne bottle, refilled their glasses.

'So...' said Sarah, glancing between the two of them, casting about for something else to say that would be innocuous. 'Philip seems very smitten with that scarlet monster of yours that he picked me up in.'

'Monster?' said Philip immediately. 'She's a beauty!'

'Her growl is terrifying!' Sarah countered, with a little laugh.

'Wait till I drive you fast in it!' Philip exclaimed. 'Then you'll hear her *roar*!'

She shuddered extravagantly, but Bastiaan addressed Philip directly. 'No,' he said firmly. 'I know you love the idea of racing around in a car that powerful, but I'm not having you smash yourself up. Or, worse, my *car*,' he added, to lighten the rejection.

A mutinous look flashed briefly across Philip's face. Sarah could see it.

'Sab would be perfectly safe with me.'

Bastiaan shook his head. Inside, his thoughts were not just on the safety of Philip driving the powerful performance car. No way was Sabine going to use *his* car to further her aims with his cousin. It was not Sabine who needed to be kept safe—it was Philip.

'Come out with me instead,' he said. 'I'll show you

its paces. We'll do the Grande Corniche. How about to-morrow?' he suggested.

Philip's face lit. 'Great!' he enthused. His expression changed. 'But…er…in the afternoon, OK?'

Bastiaan nodded. 'Yes. Do your studies in the morning, then I'll reward you with a spin after lunch.' He turned to Sabine. 'As you know,' he said deliberately, 'my cousin is here first and foremost to complete his university vacation assignments. Not to jaunt around on holiday, entertaining *you*.'

Sarah's face tightened. 'Yes, I am aware of that,' she said coolly. Did he think *she* was inciting Philip to neglect his studies? Well, all the more reason to confront him this afternoon—warn him that he needed to remove Philip yet again.

And I need Bastiaan gone too. I haven't got time for distractions—least of all by a man like this.

His gaze held hers, and for a moment, timeless and impossible, she felt as if her heart had stopped beating.

What power does he have? The question coiled in her mind like smoke. And the answer twisted in the same sinuous shape… *Too much.*

'Good,' replied Bastiaan. Her eyes had darkened in colour again. He wondered at it. Then a more potent thought overrode that. *Emeralds*, he found himself thinking—that was the jewel for her. *Emeralds with the slightest hint of aqua—at her throat, her ears…*

The vision of her draped in such jewels was instant, vivid. They would enhance her blonde beauty, catching the fire of her emerald eyes, displaying that beauty for him and him alone. He felt desire, raw and insistent, growl within him whenever he succumbed to the temptation of thinking about this beautiful, alluring woman—so unsuitable for his naive, infatuated cousin…

But for me it would be different.

Of course it would—to him she presented no danger. Sophisticated, worldly-wise, closer to his age than to Philip's… Whatever his opinion of women who sought to part impressionable young men from their money, *he* was not susceptible to such wiles. *He* was not vulnerable to a woman like her.

But she… Ah, *she* would be vulnerable to *him*. Vulnerable to the desire for him that he could read in her like a book—a desire he shared and made no attempt to conceal. Why should he? For him there was no risk in succumbing to the flame that ran between them.

He took another fortifying mouthful of champagne, making his decision. Resolution streamed within him. *Yes, he would do it!*

Long lashes dipped over his dark eyes. He reached forward across the table, moving a bowl of ripe, succulent peaches towards Sabine. 'May I entice you?' he asked. And in his eyes was an expression that in no way indicated that it was to the fruit he was referring…

Her eyes flickered. He could see it. See the hint of green fire that signalled just as much as her dilating pupils that her sexual awareness of him was radiating out on all frequencies. He smiled, drawing an answering smile from her—an instinctive response. She took a peach and he was minutely aware of the delicate length of her fingers, the pale gloss of her nails.

'Thank you,' she murmured, and dragged her gaze away from him, as though she found it difficult to do so.

He saw the heightened colour on her cheeks as she placed the peach on her plate and started to slice it diligently, head bowed a little, as if she needed to focus on her task. Her chest was rising and falling a little faster than it had been before. Bastiaan sat back, lifting his champagne glass, satisfaction in his eyes.

Philip was helping himself from the fruit bowl as well, but unlike Sarah he bit enthusiastically into the peach from his hand, spurting juice. 'These are *really* good,' he said enthusiastically.

Sarah flicked her eyes to him. 'Aren't they?' she agreed. 'Just ripe and perfect.'

She was glad to talk about the ripeness of the fruit. Glad to turn her head to Philip and talk about something else. Glad to do *anything* to drag her consciousness away from the man at the opposite end of the table. Glad, too, a few minutes later, when Paulette arrived with a tray of coffee.

Sarah started to gather up the used plates, but the housekeeper snatched them from her, muttering darkly and casting meaningful glances between her and Philip.

Surely she doesn't think I'm encouraging Philip? Sarah thought.

Another thought struck her, even more unwelcome. Did *Bastiaan* think that as well?

No, he couldn't. Of course not! She was doing her utmost to be nothing more than casually friendly— easy-going and relaxed, spending most of her time deflecting his compliments to her. A man as worldly-wise as Bastiaan Karavalas would surely be able to read her reaction to Philip's youthful ardency as easily as if she had written it large.

As easily as he must be able to read my reaction to him...

She felt her stomach clench. The knowledge that Bastiaan Karavalas could see into her feelings towards him was both dismaying and arousing. Fiercely she tried to suppress the arousal, but even as she tried she felt her eyes going to him, almost meeting his as they did so, before she continued handing plates to the unappreciative Paulette. And she felt, in that fleeting mingling before she dipped her lashes to veil her eyes, the tremor of attraction flare and catch.

He knows how he affects me—knows how he makes me feel. It's impossible to hide it from him.

A thought speared into her troubled consciousness. Coming without volition. What if *Philip* knew how attracted she was to his cousin? What if she responded openly to Bastiaan Karavalas's desire for her—hers for him? Would that destroy Philip's crush for her in an instant? Surely it would. It might be harsh, but it would be effective.

And it would give me a reason to succumb to what is happening to me.

As if standing on the edge of a precipice, she hauled herself back from the brink. Was she *insane* to think such a thing? She must be. Whether she was being Sabine or herself, whether Philip did or did not have a hopeless infatuation with her, Bastiaan Karavalas had no place in her life—*none*. Whatever the power of his sensual impact on her, she must ignore it. Suppress it. Walk away from it.

Speak to Bastiaan this afternoon—explain how he should take Philip away—and then get back to what is important. The only thing that is important to you at this time.

Making her final attempt to launch her professional career. Nothing else. *No one* else.

'Sab, did you bring your swimming costume?'

Philip's question cut across her thoughts. She looked startled. 'No—no, I didn't.'

His face fell, then brightened as Bastiaan spoke.

'No problem. There's a wide collection of assorted

swimwear in the guest suites. I'm sure there'll be something to fit you.' Bastiaan's eyes glanced over her, as if assessing her figure's size, and her eyes automatically went to his as he spoke.

'Great!' exclaimed Philip. 'When we've had coffee I'll show you where to change.'

She gave him a flickering uncertain smile. She ought to make her excuses and leave—try and have that word she needed with Bastiaan before she did so. But as she sat sipping her coffee, replete with lunch, champagne coursing gently in her veins, she had no energy to make such a move.

Her gaze slipped out over the beautiful gardens beyond the terrace. Out of nowhere she felt a different mood take hold as she committed herself to staying longer. It really was *so* beautiful here, with the gardens and the dazzlingly blue sea beyond. All she ever saw of the Côte d'Azur was the walk back to her *pension* and the local shops around the harbour. By day she was focussed only on rehearsals, by night she posed as Sabine. A relentless schedule of work. Why not relax a little now?

Why don't I make the most of being here? Who could ask for anything more lovely and enjoyable? And surely the longer I spend in Bastiaan's company the more used I'll get to him—the more immune I'll feel. The less I'll react to him.

Yes, that was the way to look at it. Extended exposure to him would surely help to dissipate this ridiculous flaring of her senses every time he glanced at her...

It was a confidence that was comprehensively annihilated as she emerged from the villa in the swimsuit Philip had found for her. Even though it was a one-piece, and she had a matching turquoise sarong wrapped around her, she burned with self-consciousness as she felt Bastiaan's eyes go straight to her from where he and Philip waited by the pool loungers.

But it was not just her own body that she was so conscious of. Nor was it the sight of Philip, his slenderly youthful physique clad in colourful board shorts with a fashionable logo, sporting snazzy wrap-around sunglasses that was causing her breath to catch. No, it was the way her eyes had gone immediately to the powerful torso of Bastiaan…to the sculpted pecs and abs, the strong biceps and wide shoulders. His hip-hugging dark blue trunks were sober compared with Philip's. His eyes were not shaded by dark glasses, and she could feel the impact of his gaze full on, even through her own sunglasses.

She made a play of making herself comfortable on a sun lounger, and then—again self-consciously—she unknotted the sarong and let it fall to either side of her, exposing her swimsuit-clad body and bare thighs.

'The bikinis didn't tempt you?'

Bastiaan's deep voice threw the question at her and Sarah gave an inner shudder at the thought of exposing even more flesh to Bastiaan Karavalas.

'They're hopeless for swimming in,' she said lightly. She relaxed her shoulders into the cushioned lounger and lifted her face to the sun. 'Oh, this is *gorgeous*,' she said feelingly, as the heat of the sun started to penetrate her skin after the cool of the interior of the house.

'Are you a sun-worshipper?' Bastiaan asked, amusement in his voice.

'When I can be,' she answered, still lightly.

'I'm surprised you're not more tanned, given that you only work nights,' he said.

She glanced towards him uncertainly. The reason she was pale was because she'd spent the first part of the summer in the north of England, teaching, and her days here were spent in rehearsal. But all she could say—again in that same deliberately light voice—was, 'I'm working on it!' Then, in order to avoid any more awkward questions, she gave a little yawn. 'Do you know, I really *do* think I might have a little siesta? Champagne at lunchtime has made me sleepy.' She slid her dark glasses off her face—no point getting white circles around her eyes—and gave a swift smile to her hosts. 'Wake me up if I start snoring,' she warned them humorously.

'You could *never* snore!' Philip said immediately, clearly aghast at the idea of his goddess doing anything so un-goddess-like.

His cousin gave a low laugh. He found that her throwaway comment, so insouciantly self-mocking, appealed to him. But then, of course, almost everything about Mademoiselle Sabine was appealing. Everything physical, at least.

Bastiaan's eyes clouded meditatively as he let his gaze rest on her slim, lissom body. Her eyes were closed, and that allowed him to study her face at leisure, while his cousin busied himself fiddling with his iPod's playlist and fishing out earphones now that the object of his admiration was so annoyingly determined to doze off.

She really is incredibly lovely to look at.

That was the thought uppermost in Bastiaan's consciousness. She had taken off her make-up, he realised, presumably to replace it with sun cream, but it had not dimmed her beauty in the least. He found himself studying her face as she lay there with her eyes studiedly closed. Curious thoughts flitted across his mind. Now she was neither *film noir* vamp nor sixties siren.

So who is she?

The question was in his mind...but he was finding no answer.

He frowned. What did it matter what image Sabine Sablon chose to present to him? What did it matter that she appeared to have an engaging sense of humour about herself? What did it matter that as she lay there, her face bare of make-up, being blessed by the sun's rays, all he could see in her was beauty...?

All he could feel was desire...?

He settled himself on his lounger and started to make his plans. The first step, he knew, must be to remove Philip from the vicinity—and for that he had an idea forming already.

Then it would be time to turn his attentions to the woman—the beautiful, alluring woman who was lying so close to him—and bring her right up close and very, *very* personal...

CHAPTER SIX

SARAH SAT, MERMAID-LIKE, on the sun-warmed rock at the sea's edge, watching Bastiaan approach her through the water with swift, powerful strokes. He and Philip were racing each other from the shore to the pontoon moored a little way off. Philip was on the pontoon now, timing Bastiaan.

She watched Bastiaan getting closer to her and tensed. She really must grab this moment to try and speak to him. She'd been looking for an opportunity since she'd woken from her siesta and they'd all headed down to the sea. So far Philip had stuck to her like glue, delighted to introduce her to the delights of the villa's private stretch of rocky shoreline and encouraging her to swim out with him to the pontoon.

As Bastiaan's long arm touched the rock and he twisted in the water, his muscles bunched to start on his return, she leant forward.

'Bastiaan…?'

It was the first time she'd addressed him by his name directly, and it sounded odd to her. Almost…*intimate*.

Dark eyes lifted to her immediately, a question in them. 'Yes?' There was impatience in his voice, and more, too.

'Can I…can I speak with you privately…before I go?'

Dark brows tugged together, then relaxed. 'Of course,'

Bastiaan said smoothly. 'I am at your service, Sabine. But not right now.'

Was he being sarcastic, ironic, or was he just in a hurry to complete his race? Maybe the latter, for he twisted his powerful torso and plunged back into his strokes, face-down in the water, threshing with fast, vigorous movement towards the pontoon.

Sarah breathed out, feeling her tension ease a tad. Well, she'd done it, but she didn't look forward to it— didn't want *any* private conversation with Bastiaan Karavalas on any subject whatsoever.

In her head, silent but piercing, came a single word. *Liar.*

An hour or so later, after a refreshing dip in the villa's pool, she announced that she needed to be going. She glanced at Bastiaan, hoping he would remember her request to speak to him.

Smoothly, he took her cue. 'Let me show you back to where you got changed,' he said.

He gestured with his arm towards the villa's interior and Sarah walked ahead of him, glad that the sarong around her was veiling her somewhat.

As they gained the marble-floored hall she heard him speak.

'So, what is it you want to say to me?'

His tone was neutral, yet Sarah felt that she could hear in its timbre a kind of subtext. She paused at the foot of the stairs and turned. Now that the moment had come she felt excruciatingly awkward. Should she *really* tell this forbidding man who had such dangerous power over her senses that his young cousin was hopelessly enamoured of her? Did he need telling in the first place? Wasn't it obvious that Philip was smitten? Maybe she didn't have to broach the subject at all—

But her cowardly hopes were dashed by the pointedly enquiring look in his dark eyes and the mordant expression in them.

She lifted her chin. 'It's about Philip—' she blurted out.

One eyebrow rose quizzically. She became crushingly conscious of his bared torso, tanned and muscular, and his still damp hip-hugging swim shorts. Of the way his wet hair was slicked back, accentuating the sculpted line of his cheekbones and jaw.

'I… I think it might be a good idea if he went…went somewhere else to complete his essays.' The words came out in a rush.

Something changed in Bastiaan's eyes. 'Why?' he asked bluntly.

She felt colour run into her cheeks, which were already hot from exposure to the sun. 'Isn't it obvious?' she returned. Her voice was husky, her words reluctant to come, resonating with the awkwardness she felt.

Long lashes dipped over deep-set eyes, and suddenly his expression was veiled.

'Ah, yes;' he said slowly. He inclined his head minutely towards her. 'Well, I shall see what I can do to accomplish what I can in that respect.' His eyes met hers. 'It may take a day or two, but I think I can see a way.'

His eyes were still holding hers, and his expression was still veiled. For a moment—just a fraction of a moment—she wondered whether she'd made her predicament plain to him.

Then he was speaking again. His tone of voice had changed. 'The bedroom you changed in is the third along the landing,' he informed her. 'Please make use of the en suite bathroom to shower and wash your hair if you wish.' Then he'd turned away and was heading back outside.

Sarah mounted the staircase with a sense of relief. It was done—she'd given Bastiaan Karavalas the warning about Philip that she'd needed to, and now she could leave him to it. Whatever plan he came up with to remove Philip from his villa and her vicinity, he would, she was pretty sure, do it effectively. Everything about him told her that he was a man who achieved everything he set himself to do. Of that she had no doubt whatsoever.

Bastiaan stood in the night-dark garden of his villa, contemplating the dim vista of the sea beyond. It was way gone midnight, but he was not tired. After Philip had driven Sabine back to the *ville*, openly thrilled to be let loose with his cousin's Ferrari again, even on the tame roads of the *Cap,* they'd both headed out to dine in Villefranche. It had been a relaxed meal, and their conversation mostly about cars, with Philip grilling him on competing makes and models and which was the absolute best amongst them all.

Bastiaan had been glad to indulge him, even though he knew that his aunt lived in terror of her son's eager enthusiasm for such powerful and potentially deadly machines—but anything that took Philip's mind off the siren charms of Sabine Sablon was to be welcomed.

Well, Philip would not be available for very much longer. Bastiaan was setting his plans in place.

He was refining them now as he stood in the cool night, with stars pricking out in the heavens and catching the swell of the sea with their trickles of light. Across the bay he could hear faint music, coming from one of the restaurants along the harbour. On his island in the Ionian there was no sound from any source other than nature.

A slight frown drew his brows together. Sabine had said how relaxing his remote island sounded—had she meant it? It was unlikely—nothing about Sabine Sablon indicated that her natural habitat was anything that resembled a small, unpopulated island where the nearest night-life was a fast speedboat away.

And yet today at the villa she had seemed happy to while away the afternoon swimming and sunbathing, openly enjoying the easy-going, lazy relaxation of it all. She had been admiring of the gardens and the sea views, appreciative of the peace and quiet, content to do nothing but let the time pass.

Confounding his expectations of her.

His expression changed. Until, of course, the very end of the afternoon. When she'd made her move on him… changing her allegiance from Philip to himself.

Bastiaan's mouth twisted. That request of hers to speak to him privately had been transparent in its objective. As transparent as her suggestion, made in an intimate husky voice, that their path would be smoother without young Philip to get in their way. Well, in that he would oblige her—and be glad to do so. For she was, of course, playing right into his hands with her suggestion.

The twist at his mouth turned into a smile. A smile of satisfaction.

Of anticipation.

Soon—very soon now—his cousin would be safe from her charms, and *he* would be enjoying them to the hilt.

Sarah's voice was low, throaty, as she finished the last number of her final set of the evening. It had been days since she'd spent the afternoon at Bastiaán Karavalas's villa, and Philip had been noticeable by his absence. He hadn't shown up at the next morning's rehearsal, and she'd picked up an apologetic text from him mid-morning, saying that he was working on his essays, then heading off with Bastiaan in the Ferrari. Nor had he turned up at the club in the evening—another apologetic text had said he was staying at Bastiaan's Monte Carlo apartment. Since then there'd been silence.

Sarah knew why—Bastiaan was doing his best to keep Philip preoccupied and away from her. She could only be grateful: it was, after all, what she'd asked him to do, and what she knew was best for Philip. For herself too.

And not just because it was keeping the disturbing impact of Bastiaan himself away from her—essential though that was for her fractured peace of mind. More than ever she needed to focus on her work. She could afford no distraction at all—not now. Least of all now.

Anxiety bit at her. She was hitting a wall—a wall that was holding her back, holding them all back, and making Max tear into her mercilessly.

They had reached the scene where the War Bride received news of her husband's death. Her aria in it was central to the drama—the fulcrum on which it turned. Although technically it was hard to sing, it was not that that was confounding her.

Max had been brutal in his criticism.

'Sarah—your husband is *dead*! A brief while ago you were rapturously in love—now all that has been ripped from you—*destroyed*! We *have* to hear that! We have to hear your despair, your disbelief. But I don't hear it! I don't hear it at *all*!'

However hard she'd tried, she hadn't been able to please him. Had not been able to get through that wall.

He'd made her sing an earlier aria, declaring her love, dazzled by the discovery of her headlong tumbling into its lightning-swift ecstasy, so that she could use it to contrast with her plunge into the depths of grief at its loss. But she still hadn't been able to please him.

'You've gone from love to grief in *days*—from bride to widow. We need to hear that unbearable journey in your voice. We need to hear it and believe it!'

She'd thrown up her hands in frustration. 'But *that's* what I can't do! I can't *believe* in it! People don't fall in love just like that only for it to end a few days later. It doesn't happen.'

In her head she remembered how she had wondered, on first hearing the tragic tale, what it must be like to love so swiftly, to hurt so badly. Unreal...quite unreal...

Her mind skittered onto pathways she should not go down.

Desire—yes. *Desire* at first sight—that was real. *That* she could not deny. Across her vision strolled Bastiaan Karavalas, with his night-dark eyes and his hooded, sensual regard that quickened her blood, heated her body. Desire had flamed in her the moment she had seen him, acknowledged his power over her...

But desire isn't love! It's not the same thing at all. Of course it isn't.

She recalled Max's exasperated rasp. 'Sarah, it's a *fable*! These characters are archetypes—timeless. They're not people you see in the street. Anton—talk to her—*make* her understand!' He'd called across to where the composer had been sitting at the piano.

But it didn't matter how much Anton went through the text with her, elucidated the way his music informed and reinforced the words she sang, she was still stuck. Still could not break through.

Max's tension cast a shadow over them all as he stepped up the intensity of their rehearsals, becoming ever more exacting. Time, as he constantly reminded them all, was running increasingly short, and their performance was not yet up to the standard it had to be.

Time and again he halted them in mid-song, demanding they repeat, improve, perfect their performance. Nerves were jittery, tempers fraying, and emotions were running high amongst them all.

Now, standing on the stage, finally lowering the microphone as she took a smattering of applause for Sabine's tedious repertoire, Sarah felt resentment fill her. Max was working them all hard, but he was working her harder than everyone else. She knew it was for her own good, for the good of her performance, the good of them all, but she was giving everything she had and it was still not enough. From somewhere, somehow, she had to find more.

Tiredness lapped at her now, and the lazy, sunlit afternoon she'd spent at the villa seemed a long time ago—far longer than a handful of days.

Memory played back the verdant flower-filled gardens, the graceful loggia and the vine-shaded terrace, the sparkling water of the pristine pool and the deep azure of the glorious Mediterranean beyond. The complete change of scene—to such a beautiful scene—had been a tonic in itself, a respite both from the rigours of rehearsal and the banal tiresomeness of performing her nightly cabaret. It had been relaxingly enjoyable despite the disturbing presence of Bastiaan Karavalas.

Because of it...

The realisation was disquieting—and yet it sent a little thrill through her at the same time. She tried to quell it. She felt it, she told herself sternly, only because she was standing here with the hot spotlight on her, in her skintight gown, just as she had been that first night when she'd felt his unknown eyes upon her.

More memories stirred. Her eyes moved briefly to the dance floor between the tables and the stage, and warmth flushed through her, as if she could still feel the firm, warm clasp of Bastiaan Karavalas's hands on her as they'd danced. Still feel the shimmering awareness of his physical closeness, the burning consciousness of her overpowering attraction to him.

An attraction she could not explain, could not cope with and certainly could not indulge .

She must not think about him—there was no point. He and Philip were both gone, and her only focus must be the festival performance ahead of her. So what was the point of the strange little pang that seemed to dart into her, twisting as it found its mark somewhere deep within? None. Bastiaan Karavalas was gone from her life and she must be glad of it.

I must!

She straightened from her slight bow, glancing out over the dining tables beyond before making ready to leave the stage.

And looked straight at Bastiaan Karavalas.

As her eyes lighted on the dark, familiar form, she felt a kick inside her that came from the same place as had that pang, only moments earlier. She hurried off the stage, aware that her heart was beating faster. *Why was he here?* Just to tell her how he'd removed Philip? Or was there another reason—a reason she would not give name to?

But Max did. 'You've lost your young, rich admirer, I see, *cherie*, and replaced him with a new one. Cultivate him—I've looked him up and he's worth a fortune!'

Sarah's jaw tightened, and she would have said something harsh, but there were tight lines of ingrained stress around Max's mouth and she could see tiredness in his face. He was working as hard as any of them—*harder*. And if she was working late nights, then so was he.

'I don't know what he's doing here,' she replied with a shrug.

Max gave his familiar waspish smile. 'Oh, come now—do you need it spelled out?'

She gave another shrug, not bothering to respond. Bastiaan thought she was Sabine—not Sarah. For a moment a thought struck her. Should she introduce Max to Bastiaan—see if he couldn't persuade him to sponsor their production? But that would mean explaining that she was Sarah, not Sabine—and all her objections to that disclosure still held. She just could not afford to let her role as Sabine contaminate her identity as an opera singer, compromise her future reputation.

'Well?' Max prompted. 'Off you go to him—it's you he's here to see, that's obvious. Like I say, be nice to him.' His eyes were veiled for a moment. 'Just don't be late for rehearsal tomorrow, OK?'

'Oh, for God's sake!' she snapped at his implication.

Whether he was joking or not, she didn't care. She was too tired to care. But if Bastiaan had taken the trouble to turn up here, she had better return the courtesy.

Max was now on his phone to Anton and she left him to it, making her way through to the front of house. Her emotions were mixed. She felt strange—both a sense of reluctance and a stirring of her blood. They warred within her.

As she approached Bastiaan's table he got to his feet. He seemed taller than ever—and suddenly more forbidding, it seemed to her, his lean body sheathed in a custom-made tuxedo. Was it because of the momentary tightening of his features? The veiling of his dark eyes? Whatever it was, she felt a shimmer go through her. Not just of an awareness that was quickening her pulse, but of its opposite as well—a kind of instinctual reserve.

She would keep this as brief as possible—it was the only sensible thing to do.

'M'sieu Karavalas,' she greeted him, with only the slightest smile at her mouth, a nod of her head.

An eyebrow lifted as he held a chair for her. 'Bastiaan, surely?' he murmured. 'Have we not advanced that far, *mademoiselle*?'

There was light mockery in his invitation to use his given name while reserving more formality for his own addressing of her. A mockery that played upon what he knew—*must* know—about her receptiveness to his masculine potency, his own appreciation of her charms...

She made no reply, merely gave a flickering social smile as she sat down while he resumed his seat.

'So, what have you done with Philip?' she asked. She kept her tone light, but this was, after all, the only reason that his cousin was here.

She saw a dark flickering cross his eyes. 'I've just returned from driving him to Paris,' he answered.

Sarah's eyes widened in surprise. *'Paris?'*

Bastiaan lifted his cognac glass. 'Yes,' he said smoothly. 'He's meeting his mother there, and visiting family friends.'

'So, how long will he be away?' she asked. She sought to keep her tone light, still, but it was hard—every nerve-ending was quivering with the overpowering impact this man had on her.

'Long enough.'

There was a hint of a drawl in his voice and it made her stare at him. She tried to quash the sudden flare in her veins as his veiled, unreadable gaze rested on her. A gaze that suddenly seared its message into her.

'And now, having disposed of the problem of my young cousin,' Bastiaan was saying, his voice dragging across her nerve-endings and making them flare with a kind of internal shiver that she felt in every cell of her body, 'we can move on to a far more interesting subject.'

Something in his face changed and he shifted slightly, relaxing back, it seemed to her, and lifting his cognac glass, his long, strong fingers curved around the bowl. His eyes rested on her with an open expression in them that was pinioning her where she sat.

She could not answer him. Could only sit, lips slightly parted, feeling her heart start to race. The rest of the room had disappeared. The rest of the *world* had disappeared. There was only her, sitting there, her body shimmering with a sensual awareness of what this man could do to her...

And then a smile flashed suddenly across his features. 'Which is, Mademoiselle Sabine, the subject of where we should dine tonight.' He paused, a light in his eyes. 'Last time you disdained my suggestion of Le Tombleur. But, tell me, does it meet with your approval tonight?'

'Tonight?' Her echo of his question was hollow, hiding the shock beneath. Hiding the sudden, overwhelming spike of adrenaline that had shot into her veins as she'd realised what he intended.

Amusement played about his well-shaped mouth. 'Do we need to wait any longer, Sabine?'

All pretence at formality was gone now. All pretence at denial of what had flared between them from the very first. There was only one reality now—coursing through her veins, pounding in her heart, sheering across her skin, quickening in her core.

This man—this man alone—who had walked into her life when she'd least expected it, least wanted it, could least afford to acknowledge it. This man who could set her pulse racing…in whose dark, disturbing presence her body seemed to come alive.

Temptation overwhelmed her. The temptation to say *Yes! Yes!* to everything he was offering. Simply to let his hand reach across the table to hers, to let him raise her to her feet, lead her from here and take her where he wanted…

To a physical intimacy, a sensual intensity, an embarkation into realms of sensuous possibility that she had never encountered before.

And why not? *Why not?* She was free, an adult and independent woman. Her emotional ties to Andrew, such as they'd been, were long gone. She was no ingénue— she knew what was being offered to her…knew it was something that would never come again in her life. For there could never be another man who would affect her the way this man could.

She could go with him as Sabine—the woman he took her to be—as assured as he in the world that this dark, powerful man moved in. A world of physical affairs that sated the body but left the heart untouched. As Sabine she could indulge in such an affair, could drink it to the full, like a glass of heady champagne that would intoxicate the blood but leave her clear-headed the following day.

The temptation was like an overpowering lure, dominating her senses, her consciousness. Then, like cold water douching down upon her, she surfaced from it.

She was not Sabine.

She was Sarah. Sarah Fareham. Who had striven all her life towards the moment that was so close now—the moment when she would walk out on stage and give the performance upon which her future life would depend.

I can't go with him—I can't.

She felt her head give a slow, heavy shake.

'*C'est impossible.*'

The words fell from her lips and her eyes were veiled beneath the ludicrously over-long false eyelashes.

His face stilled. 'Why?'

A single word. But she did not answer. Could not. Dared not. She was on a knife's edge—if she did not go now, right now, she would sever her resolve. Give in to the temptation that was lapping at her like water on a rising tide.

She shook her head again, drained her coffee cup with a hand that was almost shaking. She got to her feet. Cast one more look at him. One last look.

The man is right—the time is wrong.

'Goodnight, *m'sieu*,' she said, and dipped her head and walked away. Heading to the door beside the low stage, moving back towards her dressing room.

Behind her, Bastiaan watched her go. Then, slowly, he reached for his cognac. Emotion swelled within him but he did not know what it was. Anger? Was that it? Anger that she had defied his will for her?

Or anger that she had denied what burned between them like a hot, fierce flame?

I want her—and she denies me my desire...

Or was it incomprehension?

He did not know, could not tell—knew only that as his fingers clenched around the bowl of his cognac glass he needed the shot of brandy more than he needed air to breathe. In one mouthful he had drained it, and then, his expression changing, he pushed to his feet and left the club. Purpose was in every stride.

CHAPTER SEVEN

SARAH'S FINGERS FUMBLED with the false eyelashes as she peeled them off her eyelids, then with shaky hands wiped the caking foundation off her face, not bothering to tackle her dark eye make-up. She felt as if she was shaking on the inside, her mind shot to pieces. She'd made herself walk away from him, but it hadn't seemed to help.

All she could see in her vision was Bastiaan Karavalas, saying in his low, deep voice, 'Do we need to wait any longer?'

Emotion speared in her—a mix of panic and longing, confusion and torment. An overwhelming urge to get away as swiftly as possible, to reach the safe haven of her room in the *pension*, surged through her. She wouldn't wait to change. She simply grabbed her day clothes, stuffing them into a plastic bag and seizing up her purse, then headed for the rear exit of the club. Max was long gone and she was glad.

She stepped out into the cool night air of the little road that ran behind the club—and stopped dead.

Bastiaan's Ferrari blocked the roadway and he was propped against it, arms folded. Wordlessly he opened the passenger door.

'Give me one reason,' he said to her, 'why you will not dine with me.'

His voice was low, intense. His eyes held hers in the dim light and would not release them. She felt her mouth open to speak—but no words came out. In her head was a tumult, a jumble of thoughts and emotions and confusion.

He spoke for her. 'You can't, can you? Because this has been waiting to happen since I first set eyes on you.'

The intensity was still in his voice, in his gaze that would not let her go.

She was still trying to find the words she had to find, marshal the thoughts she had to think, but it was impossible. Impossible to do anything but succumb. Succumb to the emotions that were coursing through her. Impelling her forward. She felt one last frail, hopeless thought fleeting through her tumbling mind.

I tried—I tried to stop this happening. Tried to deny it, tried to prevent it. But I can't—I can't deny this any longer. I can't.

It was all she could manage. Then, as she sank into the low, plush seat of the powerful, sleek car, she felt herself give in entirely, completely, to what was happening. Succumbing to the temptation that was the darkly devastating man closing the door on her, lowering himself in beside her, reaching to the ignition to fire the powerful engine and moving off into the night with her at his side.

Taking her where he wanted to take her.

Where she wanted to go.

She stole a sideways look at him. Their gazes clashed. She looked away again, out over the pavements and the buildings along the roadway. She knew what she was doing—and why. Knew with every pulse of blood in her veins and in the jittering of her nerves, which were humming as if electricity were pouring through her— a charge that was coming out of the very atmosphere itself.

Enclosed as she was, only a few inches away from the long, lean body of the man next to her, she felt the low, throaty vibration of the ultra-powerful engine of the car—was aware of the sleek, luxurious interior, of the whole seductive ambience of sitting beside him.

She knew that her body was outlined by her stage dress, that her image was that of a woman in the full glamour of her beauty. And that the man beside her, clad in his hand-made tuxedo, with the glint of gold of his watch, the cufflinks in his pristine cuffs, the heady, spiced scent of his aromatic aftershave, had contrived to make the situation headily seductive.

She gave herself to it. It was too late now for anything else. Far too late.

'Where are we going?' she asked. Her voice was low-pitched and she could not quite look at him. Could not quite believe that she was doing what she was doing.

He glanced at her, with half a smile curving his sensual lips. 'I attempted once before to take you to Le Tombleur—perhaps this time you will acquiesce?'

Had there been a huskiness discernible in his voice as he'd said the word 'acquiesce'? She couldn't be sure—could only be sure that there was some kind of voltage charging her body right now, one she had never experienced before. Somewhere inside her, disappearing fast, there was a voice of protest—but it was getting feebler with every moment she was here with Bastiaan, burningly conscious of his powerful masculine presence, of the effect he had on her that she could not subdue.

Beyond the confines of the car the world was passing by. But it was far, far away from her now. Everything was far, far away.

It did not take long to get to the restaurant, set in the foothills of the Alpes-Maritimes above the crowded coastline of the Riviera. She was helped from the car, ushered inside by the tall, commanding man at her side. The *maître d'* was hurrying forward, all attention, to show them to a table out on the terrace, looking down on where the lights of the Riviera glittered like a necklace of jewels.

She eased into her seat, ultra-aware of the tightness of her gown, the voluptuousness of her figure. Her eyes went yet again to the man sitting opposite her, studying his menu. What was it about him that he could affect her the way he did? Why was she so overwhelmed by him? Why had she been so fatally tempted to succumb to what she knew she should not be doing? To dine here with him *à deux…*

And what would happen afterwards…?

Her mind skittered away. She did not think—did not dare think. Dared only to go on sitting there, occupying herself by opening the menu, glancing blindly down at the complex listings. Was she hungry? She could not tell. Could tell only that her heart rate was raised, that her skin was flushed with heat…that her eyes wanted only to go on resting on the man opposite her.

'So, what would you like to eat?'

Bastiaan's voice interrupted her hopeless thoughts and she was glad. She made herself give a slight smile. 'Something light,' she said. 'In this dress anything else is impossible!'

It had been a mistake to make such a remark, however lightly it had been said. It drew a wash of scrutiny from the dark, long-lashed eyes. She felt her colour heighten and had to fight it down by studying the menu again. She found a dish that seemed to fit the bill—scallops in a saffron sauce—and relayed it to Bastiaan. He too chose fish, but a more robust grilled monkfish, and then there followed the business of selecting wine to go with it.

Choices made, he sat back, his eyes resting on her at his leisure. Satisfaction soared through him. Her yielding had not surprised him in the least, but it had gratified him. Now, at last, he had her to himself.

His sensation of satisfaction, of the rightness of it all, increased. Yes, seducing her would, as he had always planned, achieve his goal of quashing any ambitions she might have had concerning his cousin, but as they sat there on the secluded terrace, with the night all around them, somehow his young cousin seemed very…irrelevant.

'So,' he began, 'tell me about yourself, Sabine?' It was an innocuous question—and a predictable one—but he could see a veil flicker over her eyes.

'Myself?' she echoed. 'What is there to tell that is not evident? I am a singer—what else?' She sounded flippant, unconcerned. Studiedly so.

'What part of France do you come from?' Another innocuous polite enquiry—nothing more than that. Yet once again he saw that flicker.

'Normandy,' she answered. 'A little place not far from Rouen.' Her mother's birthplace, it was the part of France she knew best, and therefore it seemed the safest answer to give.

'And have you always wanted to be a singer?'

The lift of a shoulder came again. 'One uses the talents one is given,' she replied. It was as unrevealing an answer as she could think to give.

Bastiaan's eyes narrowed minutely.

Sarah saw the narrowing. Could he tell she was being as evasive as she could? She was glad that the sommelier arrived at that moment, diverting Bastiaan. But as the man departed, and Bastiaan lifted his wine glass, she felt his dark eyes upon her again.

'To our time together,' he said, and smiled.

She made herself lift her own glass and meet his eyes. It was like drowning in dark velvet. She felt her blood quicken, her breath catch. A sense of unreality overwhelmed her—and yet this was real...vividly, pulsingly real. She was sitting here, so close to the man who could set her senses on fire with a single glance.

Oh, this was ridiculous. To be so...so overcome by this man. She *had* to claw back her composure. If she were going to take refuge in being Sabine then she must be as poised and cool as that protection provided. With an inner breath she set down her glass and then let her glance sweep out across the glittering vista far below.

'If the food is as exceptional as the location, I can understand why this place has such a reputation,' she murmured. It seemed a safe thing to say—and safe things were what she was clutching at.

'I hope both please you,' he replied.

His lashes dipped over his eyes. It was clear to him that she did not wish to talk about herself, but her very evasiveness told him what he wanted to know—that she was, indeed, a woman who presented to the world what she chose to present. For himself, he did not care. Sabine Sablon would not, after all, be staying long in his life.

'Does this have a Michelin star yet?' Sarah asked, bringing her gaze back to him. Another safe thing to ask.

'One. But a second is being targeted,' he answered.

'What makes the difference, I wonder?' Sarah asked. Safe again...

He lifted his wine glass. Talking about Michelin stars was perfectly acceptable as a topic. It lasted them until their food arrived, and then they moved on to the subject of the Côte d'Azur itself—how it had changed and developed, what its charms and attractions were.

It was Bastiaan who talked most, and he soon became aware that Sabine was adept at asking questions of him, keeping the conversation flowing.

And all the time, like a deep, powerful current in a river on whose surface aimless ripples were circling, another conversation was taking place. One that was wordless, silent, yet gaining strength with every politely interested smile, every nod, every lift of a fork, of a glass, every glance, every low laugh, every gesture of the hand, every shift in body position…every breath taken.

It was a conversation that could lead to only one end… take them to only one destination.

The place he had determined she should go. The place she could no longer resist him taking her to.

Sarah climbed back into the car and Bastiaan lowered his tall frame into the driving seat beside her. Immediately the space confining them shrank. Her mind was in a daze. Wine hummed in her veins—softening her body so that it seemed to mould to the contours of the leather seat. She heard the throaty growl of the engine and the powerful car moved forward, pressing her further into her seat. She could feel the low throb of her beating heart, the flush of heat in her skin.

But it was in *Sabine's* breast that her heart was beating. It was Sabine whose senses were dominated by the presence of this magnetic, compelling man beside her. Sabine who was free to do what she was doing now—ignoring everything in the world except this man, this night…

Sabine, alluring, sensual and sophisticated, could yield to the overpowering temptation that was Bastiaan Karavalas and all that he promised. Sabine had led her to this place, this time, this moment—a moment that Sabine would wish to come…would choose to be in…

This is going to happen. It is going to happen and I am not going to stop it. I want it to happen.

She did. It might be rash, it might be foolish, it might be the thing she had least expected would happen during this summer, but she *was* going to go with Bastiaan Karavalas.

This night.

And as for tomorrow…

She would deal with that then. Not now.

Now there was only her, and him, and being taken to where he was taking her. Wordless. Voiceless. Irreversible.

He took her to his apartment in Monte Carlo.

It was as unlike the villa on Cap Pierre as she could imagine. In a modern high-rise block, its decor sleek and contemporary. She stood by the huge-paned glass windows, gazing out over the marina far below, seeing the glittering lights of the city scintillating like diamonds, feeling the rich sensuality of her body, the tremor in her limbs.

Waiting…

Waiting for the man standing behind her, his presence, his scent overpowering her. Waiting for him to make his move…to take her into his arms…his embrace…his bed.

She heard him murmur something, felt the warmth of his breath on the nape of her neck, the drift of his hands around her shoulders, so light, feather-light, and yet with a silken power that made her breath catch, her lips part as the tremor in her limbs intensified. She felt the powerful touch of his palms glide down her bare arms, fasten on her wrists, and with a movement as subtle as it was irresistible, she felt him turn her towards him.

She lifted her face to him, lips parted, eyes deep and lustrous. She was so close she could feel the strength and heat of his body, feel the dark intensity of his gaze, of those eyes holding hers, conveying to her all that she knew was in her own eyes as well.

He smiled. A slow pull of his mouth. As if he knew what she was feeling, as if he were colluding with the strange, strong, heavy pulse of the blood in her veins. His eyes worked over her face leisurely, taking in every contour, every curve of her features.

'You are so beautiful…' It was a husky statement. 'So very beautiful…'

For one long, timeless moment his eyes poured into hers as they stood there, face to face, and then his hands closed around her slender, pliant waist and drew her to him slowly, very slowly, as if each increase in the pressure of his hands drawing her to him was almost against his will and yet as impossible for him to resist as it was for her to resist.

Nor did she want to—she wanted only to feel his mouth making its slow descent to hers, wanted him to fuse his lips to hers, to take her mouth, possess it, mould it to his, open it to his…

And when he did her eyes could only close, her throat could only sigh with a low sound of absolute pleasure, as with skill and sensual slowness his mouth found hers to take it and taste it. Somewhere inside her, very dimly, she could feel heat pooling. Her heart seemed to cease its beating as she felt the rich, sensual glide of his lips on hers, his mouth opening hers to him, his kiss deepening.

His hold on her waist tightened, strengthened, as the shift of his stance changed so that she was being cradled against him, and with a little shimmer of shocked response she felt how aroused he was.

His arousal fired hers so that her blood surged, her breath caught, the melding of her mouth to his quickened and deepened. Her hands lifted, closing around the strong breadth of his back, splaying against the smooth fabric of his dinner jacket. She felt her breasts crush against the wall of his chest. She heard his low growl, felt his palms pull her tighter against him.

Excitement flared through her. Every cell in her body was alive, sensitive, eager for more of what she was already experiencing. And then, as if on a jerking impulse, he swept her body into his arms, as if she were nothing more than a feather. He was striding away with her, his mouth still fastened upon hers, and the world beyond whirled as he deposited her heavily upon the cold satin surface of a wide, soft bed and came down beside her.

His mouth continued devouring hers, and one thigh was thrown over her as a kind of glory filled her. Desire, open and searing, flooded her. She felt her breasts tighten and tingle and threw back her head to lift them more. Another low growl broke from him, and then her arms were being lifted over her head and pinioned with one hand while his palm closed possessively over the sweet, straining mound of her breast. She gasped with pleasure, groaning, her head moving restlessly from side to side, her mouth, freed from his, abandoned and questing.

Was this her? Could it be her? Lying like this, flaming with a desire that was consuming her, possessing her, shameless and wanton?

His heavy thigh lay between hers and she felt her hips writhe against it, wanting more and yet more of the sensations that were being loosened within her. Did she speak? And if she did, what did she say? She did not know—knew only that she must implore him to bestow upon her what she was craving, yearning for, more and more and more…

Never had she felt like this, so deeply, wildly aroused. As if she were burning with a flame that she had never known.

He smiled down at her. 'I think it is time, *cherie*, that we discarded these unnecessary clothes…'

He jack-knifed to his feet, making good on his words. She could not move—could only gaze at him in the dim light as he swiftly, carelessly, disposed of what he was wearing. And then his hard, lean body was lowering down beside her, his weight indenting the mattress. She felt his nakedness like a brand, and suddenly, out of nowhere, her cheeks were flaring, her eyelids veiling him from her sight.

He gave a low, amused laugh. 'Shy?' he murmured. 'At *this* point?'

She couldn't answer him—could only let her eyes flutter open. And for an instant—just an instant—she thought she saw in the dim light a question suddenly forming in his…

But then it was gone. In its place a look of deep, sensual appreciation.

'You are beautiful indeed, *cherie*, as you are…but I want to see your beauty *au naturel*.'

A hand lifted to her shoulders, easing the straps away first on one side, then the other. With a kind of sensual delicacy he peeled her gown down her body to her waist, letting his gaze wander over her in that lazy, leisurely fashion that made the heat pool in her body. Then he tugged it further still, over her hips, taking with it her panties, easing the material down her thighs to free her legs. Now only her stockings remained, and with a sense of shock she realised what it was he was seeing of her…

'Shall I make love to you like this?' he asked, and there was still that lazy, sensual amusement in his voice.

She answered him. No, she would *not* be arrayed like that for him.

With swift decision she sat up, peeling her stockings from her body, tossing them aside with the belt that fastened them. Her hair was tumbling now, free and lush over her breasts, as she sat looking at him where he lay back on the coverlet, blatant in his own nakedness. She gazed down at him, pushing back her hair with one hand. He was waiting—assured, aroused, confident—conspiring with her to make the next move, and she was glad to do so.

Draping her long hair around one shoulder, she leant forward. Her breasts almost grazed his bared chest as she planted her hands either side of him.

'Where shall I start?' she heard herself murmur, with the same warm, aroused amusement in her voice as his had held.

An answering amusement glittered in his dark eyes. 'Take me,' he said, and the amusement was there in his deep voice too. 'I am yours.'

She gave a low, brief laugh, and then her mouth was gliding, skimming over the steel-hard contours of his chest. Lightly…arousingly.

For interminable moments he endured it, his arousal mounting unbearably, as she deliberately teased and tempted him. And then, with an explosive edge, he knew he could take it no longer. He hauled her down on him—fully on him—and the satisfaction he knew as he heard her gasp was all he needed to hear. He rolled her over beneath him, and with a thrust of his thigh parted her.

His mouth found hers—claiming and clinging, feasting and tasting. Urgency filled him. He wanted her *now*.

Almost he succumbed to the overwhelming urge to possess her as she was. But that would be madness—insanity. With a groan of self-control he freed himself, flung out an arm sideways and reached into the bedside drawer.

She was seeking to draw him back, folding her hands around him, murmuring, and he could hear the breathless moans in her throat as she sought him.

'Wait—a moment only...'

It was almost impossible for him to speak. His arousal was absolute...his body was in meltdown. He *had* to have her—he *had* to possess her. Had to complete what he had wanted to do from the very first moment of laying eyes upon her lush, alluring body, since he had first felt the response in those emerald eyes...

Oh, she might be as mercenary as he feared, as manipulative as he suspected, but none of that mattered. Only this moment mattered—this urgency, this absolute overriding desire for her that was possessing him.

A moment later he was ready, and triumph surged through him. At last he could take what he wanted—possess *her*, this woman who would belong to no one else but him...

She was drawing him down on her, her thighs enclosing his as her body opened to him, and with a relief that flooded through him he fused his body deep, deep within her own...

Immediately, like a firestorm, sensation exploded within him and he was swept away on burning flames that consumed him in a furnace of pleasure. For an instant so brief he was scarcely conscious of it, he felt dismay that he had not waited for her. But then, with a reeling sense of amazed wonder, he realised that she had come with him into the burning flames...that she was clinging to him and crying out even as he was, and that their bodies were wreathed in a mutual consummation that was going on and on and on...

Never before had he experienced such a consummation. Never in all his wide and varied experience had the intensity been like this. It was as if his whole mind and body and being had ignited into one incredible, endless sensation—as if their bodies were melding together, fusing like molten metal into each other.

When did it change? When it did it start to ebb, to take him back down to the plane of reality, of consciousness? He didn't know—couldn't say. Could only feel his body shaking as it returned slowly, throbbingly, to earth. His lungs were seizing and he could feel his heart still pounding, hear his voice shaking as he lifted himself slightly from her, aware that his full weight was crushing her.

He said something, but he did not know what.

She was looking at him—gazing up with an expression in her eyes that mirrored what he knew was in his own. A kind of shock. She was stunned by what had happened.

For one long moment they seemed just to stare at each other disbelievingly. Then, with a ragged intake of breath, Bastiaan managed to smile. Nothing more than that. And he saw her eyes flutter closed, as if he had released her. A huge lassitude swept over him, and with a kind of sigh he lowered himself again, settling her sideways against him, pulling her into his warm, exhausted body.

Holding her so close against him was wonderful, reassuring, and all that he wanted. His hands spread across her silken flanks, securing her against him, and he heard her give a little sigh of relaxation, felt one of her hands close over his, winding her fingers into his, and then, with a final settling of her body, she was still, her breathing quietening as she slipped into sleep.

In his final moment of remaining consciousness Bastiaan reached back to haul the coverlet over them both and then, when they were cocooned beneath, he wrapped his arm around her once more and gave himself to sleep, exhausted, replete, and in that moment possessing all that he wanted to possess on earth.

Something woke her—she wasn't sure what. Whatever it was, it had roused her from the deep slumber into which she'd fallen…a slumber deeper and sweeter than she had ever known.

'Good morning.'

Bastiaan, clad in a towelling robe, was looking down at her. His dark eyes were drinking her in. She did not answer. Could not. Could only hear in her head the words that had forced their way in.

What have I done? Oh, God, what have I done?

But she didn't need to ask—the evidence was in her naked body, in her lying in the bed of Bastiaan Karavalas.

Memory burned like a meteor, scorching through the sky. Awareness made her jack-knife. 'Oh, God—what time is it?' She stared at him, horror-struck.

His face pulled into a frown. 'Of what significance is that?' he demanded.

But she did not answer him—did not do anything except leap from the bed, not caring that she was naked. Not caring about anything except snatching, from wherever she could see them, her clothes from the previous night.

Dismay and horror convulsed her. She pushed into the bathroom, caught sight of herself in the huge mirror, and gave a gasping groan. Three minutes later she stumbled out—looking ludicrous, she knew, with her tangled hair tumbling over her shoulders, her evening dress from the night before crumpled and idiotic on her. But she didn't care—couldn't care. Couldn't afford to care.

She might be wearing Sabine's clothes, left over from the night before, but Sabine herself was gone. Sarah was back—and she was panicking as she had never panicked before.

'What the *hell*...?' Bastiaan was staring at her.

'I have to go.'

'*What?* Don't be absurd.'

She ignored him. Pushed right past him out into the reception room and stared desperately around, looking for her bag. Dimly she remembered that her day clothes were in a plastic bag that must, she thought urgently, still be in the footwell of Bastiaan's car. But there was no time for that now. No time for anything except to get out of here and find a bus stop...

Oh, God, it will take for ever to get back. I'll be late— so late. Max will be furious!

She felt her arm caught, her body swung round. 'Sabine—what is going on? Why are you running away?'

She stared, eyes blank with incomprehension. 'I have to go,' she said again.

For a second there was rejection in his eyes, and then, as if making a decision, he let her go.

'I'll call a cab—' he said.

'No!'

He ignored her, crossed to a phone set by the front door, spoke swiftly to someone she assumed was the concierge. Then he hung up, turned to look at her.

'I don't know what is going on, or why. But if you insist on leaving I cannot stop you. So—go.' His voice was harsh, uncomprehending. His expression blank.

For one timeless moment she was paralysed. Could

only stare at him. Could only feel as if an explosion was taking place inside her, detonating down every nerve, along every vein.

'Bastiaan, I—'

But she could not speak. There was nothing to say. She was not Sabine. She was Sarah. And she had no place here…no place at all…

He opened the front door for her and she stumbled through.

As she ran for the elevator she heard the door slam behind her. Reverberating through every stricken cell in her body.

CHAPTER EIGHT

BASTIAAN WAS DRIVING. Driving as though he were being chased by the hounds of hell. The road snaked up, high into the Alpes-Maritimes, way beyond the last outpost of the Riviera and out into the hills, where bare rock warred with the azure skies. Further on and further up he drove, with the engine of the car roaring into the silence all around him.

At the top of the pass he skidded to the side, sending a scree of stones tumbling down into the crevasse below. He cut the engine but the silence brought no peace. His hands clenched over the steering wheel.

Why had she run from him? *Why?* What had put that look of absolute panic on her face?

Memory seared across his synapses. What had flamed between them had been as overwhelming for her as it had been for him—he knew that. Knew it with every male instinct he possessed. That conflagration of passion had set them both alight—*both* of them.

It has never been like that for me before. Never.

And she had gazed at him with shock in her eyes, with disbelief.

Had she fled because of what had happened between them? Had it shocked her as it had shocked him? So that she could not handle it, could not cope with it?

*Something is happening, Sabine, between us—
something that is not in your game plan. Nor in mine.*

He stared out over the wide ravine, an empty space
into which a single turn of the wheel would send his car—
himself—hurtling. He tried to make himself think about
Philip, about why he had come here to rescue him from
Sabine Sablon, but he could not. It seemed...irrelevant.
Unimportant.

There was only one imperative now.

He reached for the ignition, fired the engine. Nosed
the car around and headed back down to the coast with
only one thought in his head, driving him on.

Max lifted his hand to halt her. 'Take it again,' he said.
His voice was controlled, but barely masking his exas-
peration.

Sarah felt her fingers clench. Her throat was tight,
and her shoulders and her lungs. In fact every muscle in
her body felt rigid. It was hopeless—totally, absolutely
hopeless. All around her there was a tension that was
palpable. Everyone present was generating it, feeling it.
She most of all.

When she'd arrived at rehearsal, horrendously late,
Max had turned his head to her and levelled her with a
look that might have killed her, like a basilisk's. And then
it had gone from bad to worse...to impossible.

Her voice had gone. It was as simple and as brutal as
that. It didn't matter that Max wasn't even attempting to
get her to sing the aria—she could sing nothing. Nothing at all.

But it was not the mortification of arriving so late to
rehearsal, her breathless arrival and hectic heartbeat that
were making it impossible for her to sing. It was because

inside her head an explosion had taken place, wiping out everything that had once been in it.

Replacing it only with searing white-hot memory.

Her night with Bastiaan.

It filled her head, overwhelming her, consuming her consciousness, searing in her bloodstream—every touch, every caress, every kiss. Impossible to banish. Impossible for anything else to exist for her.

'Sarah!' Max's voice was sharp, edged with anger now.

She felt another explosion within her. 'I *can't.*' The cry broke from her. 'I just can't! It isn't there—I'm sorry... I'm *sorry*!'

'What the hell use is sorry?' he yelled, his control clearly snapping.

And suddenly it was all too much. Just too much. Her late arrival and the collapse of her voice were simply the final straw.

Alain, her tenor, stepped forward, put a protective arm around her shoulder. 'Lay off her, Max!' he snapped.

'And lay off the rest of us too!' called someone else.

'Max, we're exhausted. We *have* to have a break.'

The protests were mounting, the grumbling turning into revolt. For a dangerous moment Max looked as if he wanted to yell at them all, then abruptly he dropped his head.

'OK,' he said. 'Break, everyone. Half an hour. Get outside. Fresh air.'

The easing of the fractured tension was palpable and the company started to disperse, talking in low, relieved voices.

Alain's hand dropped from Sarah's shoulder. 'Deep breaths,' he said kindly, and wandered off to join the general exodus outdoors.

But Sarah couldn't move. She felt nailed to the floor. She shut her eyes in dumb, agonised misery.

Dear God, hadn't she said she must have no distractions. *None*. And then last night—!

What have I done? Oh, what have I done!

It was the same helpless, useless cry she'd given as she'd stood in Bastiaan's apartment naked, fresh from his bed.

Anguish filled her—and misery.

Then, suddenly, she felt her hands being taken.

'Sarah, look at me,' said Max.

His voice had changed—his whole demeanour had changed. Slowly, warily, she opened her eyes. His expression was sympathetic. Tired lines were etched around his eyes.

'I'm sorry,' he said. 'We're all burning out and I'm taking it out on you—and you don't deserve it.'

'I'm so sorry for arriving late,' she replied. 'And for being so useless today.'

But Max squeezed her hands. 'You need a break,' he said. 'And more than just half an hour.'

He seemed to pause, searching her strained expression, then he nodded and went on.

'Should I blame myself?' he asked. There was faint wry humour in his dry voice. 'Wasn't I the one who told you not to be late this morning? Knowing who'd turned up to see you? No, no, *cherie*—say nothing. Whatever has happened, it's still going on in your head. So…'

He took a breath, looking at her intently.

'What I want you to do is…go. Go. Whatever it takes—do it. I don't want to see you again this week. Take a complete break—whether that's to sob into your pillow or… Well, whatever! If this rich cousin of Philip is good for you, or bad, the point is that *he's* in your head and your work is not.' His voice changed. 'Even without last night you've hit the wall, and I can't force you through it. So you must rest, and then—well, we shall see what we shall see.'

He pressed her hands again, his gaze intent.

'Have faith, Sarah—have faith in yourself, in what you can accomplish. You are so nearly there! I would not waste my genius on you otherwise,' he finished, with his familiar waspish humour.

He stepped back, patting her hands before relinquishing them.

'So—go. Take off. Do anything but sing. Not even Sabine's dire ditties. I'll sort it with Raymond—somehow.'

He dropped a light kiss on her forehead.

'*Go!*' he said.

And Sarah went.

Bastiaan nosed the car carefully down the narrowing street towards the harbour. She was here somewhere—she had to be. He didn't know where her *pension* was, but there were a limited number, and if necessary he would check them all out. Then there was the nightclub as well—someone there at this time of day would know where she might be.

I have to find her.

That was the imperative driving him. Conscious thought was not operating strongly in him right now, but he didn't care. Didn't care that a voice inside his head was telling him that there was no reason to seek her out like this. One night with her had been enough to achieve his ends—so why was he searching for her?

He did not answer—refused to answer. Only continued driving, turning into the area that fronted the harbour, face set, eyes scanning around as if he might suddenly spot her.

And she was there.

He felt his blood leap, his breath catch.

She was by the water's edge, seated on a mooring bollard, staring out to sea. He felt emotions surge through him—triumph shot through with relief. He stopped the car, not caring whether it was in a parking zone or not. Got out. Strode up to her. Placed a hand on her shoulder.

'Sabine…' His voice was rich with satisfaction. With possession.

Beneath his hand he felt her whole body jump. Her head snaked around, eyes widening in shock.

'Oh, God…' she said faintly.

He smiled. 'You did not truly believe I would let you go, did you?' he said. He looked down at her. Frowned suddenly. 'You have been crying,' he said.

There was disbelief in his voice. Sabine? Weeping? He felt the thoughts in his head rearrange themselves. Felt a new one intrude.

'What has made you cry?' he demanded. It was not *him*—impossible that it should be him.

She shook her head. 'It's just…complicated,' she said.

Bastiaan found himself hunkering down beside her, hands resting loosely between his bunched thighs, face on a level with hers. His expression was strange. His emotions stranger. The Sabine who sat here, her face tear-stained, was someone new—someone he had never seen before.

The surge of possessiveness that had triumphed inside him a moment ago on finding her was changing into something he did not recognise. But it was moving within him. Slowly but powerfully. Making him face this new emotion evolving within him.

'No,' he contradicted, and there was something in his voice that had not been there before. 'It is very simple.' He looked at her, his eyes holding hers. 'After last night, how could it be anything else?'

His gaze became a caress and his hand reached out softly to brush away a tendril of tangled hair that had escaped from its rough confines in a bunched pleat at the back of her head. He wanted to undo the clasp, see her glorious blond mane tumble around her shoulders. Although what she was wearing displeased him, for it seemed to be a shapeless tee shirt and a pair of equally shapeless cotton trousers. And her face was blotchy, her eyes strained.

Yet as he spoke, as his hand gently brushed the tendril from her face, he saw her expression change. Saw the strain ebb from her eyes, her blotched skin re-colour.

'I don't know why you ran from me,' he heard himself say, 'and I will not ask. But…' His hand now cupped her chin, feeling the warmth of her skin beneath his fingertips. 'This I *will* ask.'

His eyes rested on hers—his eyes that had burned their way into hers in the throes of exquisite passion. But now they were simply filled with a single question. The only one that filled his head, his consciousness.

'Will you come with me now? And whatever complications there are will you leave them aside?'

Something shifted in her eyes, in the very depths of them. They were green—as green as emeralds. Memory came to him. He remembered how he'd wanted to drape her in emeralds. It seemed odd to him just then. Irrelevant. Unimportant. Only one thing was important now.

The answer she was giving him with her beautiful, emerald-green eyes, which were softening even as he held them. Softening and lightening and filling with an expression that told him all he needed to know.

He smiled again. Not in triumph this time, nor in possession. Just smiled warmly upon her.

'Good,' he said. Then he drew her to her feet. His smile deepened. 'Let's go.'

He led her to his car and helped her in.

The rest of this week, thought Sarah.

The wealth of time seemed like largesse of immense proportions. The panic that had been in her breast and the tension that had bound her lungs with iron, her throat with barbed wire, were gone. Just...*gone*. They had fallen from her as she had risen to her feet, had her hand taken by Bastiaan. Her feet felt like cushions of air.

I've been set free!

That was what it felt like. As if she had been set free from all the complications that had been tearing into her like claws and teeth ever since she'd surfaced that morning, realizing what she'd done. What *she*—Sarah, not Sabine—had done. And now... Oh, now, it didn't matter—didn't matter who she was.

Max understood—understood the entire impossibility of what had been tying her in knots for days now, ever since Bastiaan Karavalas had walked into her life.

Right man—wrong time.

But no more—not for a precious handful of glorious, wonderful, liberating days.

I can do what I've been longing to do—what I succumbed to doing last night. This man alone is different from any I've ever known. What happened last night was a revelation, a transformation.

She quivered with the memory of their passion as he

started the car, gunning the engine. She turned to look at him, her eyes as bright as stars.

'Where are we going?' she asked.

She had asked that last night and he had taken her to a new, glittering realm of enchantment and desire, passion and fulfilment.

'My villa,' he answered, his eyes warm upon her before he glanced back to steer the car out of the little town, along the road that curved towards the *Cap*.

Gladness filled her. The apartment in Monte Carlo was glitzy and glamorous, but it did nothing for her. It was his villa that charmed her.

'Wonderful...' she breathed. She felt as light as air, floating way, way up into the sky—the carefree, bright blue sky, where there were no complications to tether her down.

I'm free from everything except seizing with both hands this time now! Right man—right time. Right now!

Her spirits soared, and it seemed they were at the villa in minutes. For a brief interlude Sarah felt self-conscious about encountering Paulette again. If the woman had considered her a threat to Philip, what might she think of her cavorting with her employer? But Paulette, she discovered, had a day off.

'So we'll have to make our own lunch,' Bastiaan told her.

He didn't want to make lunch—he wanted to make love. But his stomach was growling. He was hungry. Hungry for food, hungry for her. He would sate both appetites and life would be good. *Very* good.

He had Sabine back with him, and right now that was all he wanted.

As he headed towards the kitchen he glanced out of the French windows to the terrace beyond. Only a few days ago they had lunched there, all three of them—he and Sabine and Philip.

It seemed a long time ago.

'So…' Bastiaan set down his empty coffee cup on the ironwork table on the villa's shady terrace and leant back in his chair, his eyes resting on Sabine. 'What shall we do now?'

The expression in his eyes made it totally clear what he would like to do—he'd sated his hunger for food, and now he wanted to sate a quite different hunger.

Across from him, Sarah felt her pulse give a kick—when Bastiaan looked at her like that it was hard to respond in any other way. Lunch had been idyllic. Simple *charcuterie* and *fromage*, with huge scarlet tomatoes and more of the luscious peaches they'd had the other day. It had felt a little odd to be here again, receiving such intimacy from Bastiaan.

Has it really happened? Am I really here with Bastiaan, and are we lovers?

But it was true—it really was—and for the rest of this glorious week it could go on being true.

A rich, sensuous languor swept through her as his gaze twined with hers. A wicked sparkle glinted in her own.

'The pool looks irresistible…' she murmured provocatively.

She almost heard him growl with frustration, but gallantly he nodded. 'It does indeed—especially with you in it.' His eyes glinted too. 'Do you want me to guide you back to the room you changed in last time? Or—' and now there was even more of a wickedly intimate glint in his eyes '—shall we dispense with swimsuits altogether?'

She laughed in answer, and disappeared off to change.

Maybe they could go skinny-dipping at night, under the stars…?

The water was wonderfully refreshing, and so was Bastiaan's company. There was a lot of playful frolicking, and from her more covert—and not so covert—appreciation of his strong, muscled physique. A thrill went through her. For now—for this brief, precious time—he was hers. How wonderful was that?

Very wonderful—and more than wonderful: incredible.

It was incredible when, on retiring to the bedroom in the villa to shower in the en-suite bathroom, she discovered Bastiaan could wait no longer.

He stepped inside the shower, hands slicking down her wet, tingling body. She gasped in shock and then in arousal as skilfully, urgently and devastatingly he took possession of her. As her legs wrapped around him and he lifted her up her head fell back in ecstasy, and it seemed to her that she had been transformed into a different person. A person who was neither the sultry Sabine nor the soprano Sarah, but someone whose only existence was to meld herself with this incredible, sensual male, to fuse her body with his, to burn with him in an explosion of physical pleasure and delight.

Afterwards, as they stood exhausted, with the cooling water streaming over them, her breath coming in hectic pants, he cut the shower, reached for huge fleecy towels and wrapped her up as if she were a precious parcel.

He let his hands rest over her damp shoulders, his eyes pouring down into hers. 'What do you do to me?' he asked. There was a strange quality in his voice, a strange expression in his dark eyes.

She let her forehead rest on his chest, the huge lassitude of the aftermath of passion consuming her now.

She could not answer him for it was a question that was in her own being too.

He swung her up into his arms, carried her through into the bedroom, lowering her down upon the cool cotton coverlet, coming down beside her. He drew her into his sheltering embrace, kissed her nape with soft, velvet kisses. And then exhausted, sated, complete, they slept.

When they awoke they made love again, slowly and softly, taking their time—all the time in the world—in the shuttered late-afternoon light of the cool room. And this time Bastiaan brought her to a different kind of ecstasy—a slow, blissful release that flowed through her body like sweet water after drought.

Afterwards they lay a little while in each other's loose embrace, and then Bastiaan lifted his head from the pillow.

'I know,' he told her, 'a great way to watch the sunset.'

It was indeed, Sarah discovered, a wonderful way to watch the sunset.

He took her out to sea in a fast, sleek motor launch that they boarded from the little quay at the rocky shore below the villa. Exhilaration filled her as Bastiaan carved a foaming wake in the darkening cobalt water, the sun low on the surface, turning the Mediterranean to gold as it kissed the swell.

He cut the engine, letting the silence settle around them, and she sat next to him, his arm casually around her shoulder, his body warm against hers. She could feel the gentle bob of the waves beneath the hull, feel the warmth of the sun on her face as she lifted it to its lingering rays. It was as if they were the only people in the world. Here out on the water, with Bastiaan's arm around her, she felt as if all that lay beyond had ceased to be.

Here there were no complications.

Here there was only Bastiaan.

What is happening to me?

The question wound in her mind between the circuits of her thoughts, seeking an answer she was not ready to find. It was far easier simply to go on sitting there, with the warm air like an embrace, the hugeness of the sea all around them, the rich gold of the setting sun illuminating them. This—now—was good. This was all she wanted. This was her contentment.

They headed back to shore in the gathering dusk.

'Would you like to eat out or at the villa?' Bastiaan asked.

'Oh, don't go out,' she said immediately. Then frowned. 'But I'm not very good at cooking, and I don't want you to have to…' she said uncertainly. Could a man like Bastiaan Karavalas really cook a meal?

He gave a laugh. 'We'll have something delivered,' he told her. 'What would you like?'

'Pizza?' she suggested.

He laughed again. 'Oh, I think we can do better than that,' he said.

And indeed they could.

On the Côte d'Azur, when money was no object, it seemed that gourmet meals could be conjured out of thin air.

As she took her place at the table on the terrace, in the warm evening air, it was to discover that a team of servers had arrived from a nearby Michelin-starred restaurant and were setting out their exquisite wares.

She and Bastiaan had already shared a glass of champagne before the meal arrived, and she felt its effervescence in her veins. Now, as the team from the restaurant departed, Bastiaan lifted a glass of rich, ruby Burgundy.

'To our time together,' he said. It was the same toast he'd given the night before, at Le Tombleur.

Sarah raised her own glass.

Our time together...these few precious days...

She felt emotion pluck at her.

From his seat, Bastiaan rested his eyes on her. She looked nothing like she had the night before when they had dined. And he was glad of it. She was wearing a pale blue kimono that he had found in a closet. In sheerest silk, it was knotted at the waist and had wide sleeves, a plunging neckline that gave the merest hint of the sweet swell of her breasts. Her glorious hair was loose, cascading down her back. She wore no make-up. Needed not a scrap of it.

How beautiful she is. How much I desire her!

He tried to remember why it was he had seduced her. Tried to remember his fears for Philip. Tried to remember how he had determined to foil her machinations. But his memory seemed dim. Flawed.

As he gazed on her they seemed unreal, those fears. Absurd...

Did I misjudge her?

That was the question that uncoiled itself in his mind. The question that pressed itself against his consciousness. The question which, with every passing moment he spent with her, seemed more and more...*unnecessary.*

Thoughts flitted through his mind. What evidence, after all, *was* there against her? Oh, Philip was lovestruck—that was undeniable. His every yearning gaze told Bastiaan that. But what of her? What of her behaviour towards Philip?

I thought her nothing more than a blatant gold-digger—trying to exploit Philip's youth and vulnerability. But is she—was she?

I thought that she had blatantly switched her attentions to me—had manoeuvred me to get rid of Philip from the scene.

But why, then, had she been so reluctant to go with him when he'd sought her out on his return from Paris? And why had she fled from him in his apartment that first morning? If she'd been no better than he'd thought her, wanting him for his wealth, she should have clung to him like glue. Not wept by the quayside while he'd searched so urgently for her.

Was that the behaviour of the woman he'd thought her to be? It couldn't be—it just *couldn't*.

There is no evidence against her. From the very start she has confounded my suspicions of her—time after time. All I have to go on, other than my fears for Philip, is that payment that he made.

That was the truth of it. Had he been conjecturing everything else about her? Feeding his suspicions simply because he'd wanted to protect his young cousin? He took a breath, fixed his eyes on her as she lifted her wine glass to answer his toast, looked across at him and smiled—her eyes like incandescent jewels, rich and glowing.

Emotion leapt in him, and in his head he heard his own voice, searing across his thoughts.

There could be an explanation for why Philip paid out that money. All I have to do is ask him. There is no reason—none—to fear that it was to Sabine. She could be completely innocent of the suspicions I've had of her.

As innocent as he wanted her to be. Wanted so much for her to be…

'To us,' he said, and let his eyes mingle and meld with hers—the eyes of this woman who could be everything he wanted her to be. And nothing he did not.

From this moment on he would not let his fears, his

suspicions, poison him. Would not let anything spoil his enjoyment of this moment, this time with her.

And nothing did—that was the bliss of it. Cocooned with her at the villa, he made love to her by day and by night—and *every* time it took him by storm. A storm not only of the senses but of something more.

What is it you do to me?

That was the question that came every time she lay cradled in his arms, her head on his chest, her arm like a silken bond around his waist, her body warm and flushed with passion spent.

The question had no answer—and soon he did not seek an answer. Soon he was content simply to let the hours pass with her. Time came and went, the sun rose and set, the stars wheeled in the clear sky each night as they lay out on the pool loungers, gazing upwards, hand in hand, the cool midnight breeze whispering over their bodies, the moon rising to cast its silver light upon them.

Who *was* this woman? Bastiaan asked of himself, thinking of all that he knew of her. It no longer seemed to matter. Not any more.

Sometimes he caught fragments of her life—a passing mention of the garden at a house in Normandy where, so he surmised, she must have grown up. The climate and the terrain so different from this sun-baked southern shore. Once he tried to draw her out about her singing, but she only shook her head and changed the subject with a smile, a kiss.

Nor did she talk to him about *his* life—only asked him about Greece. How it was to live there, with so much history, the history of millennia, pressing all around him. Of how he made his money, his wealth, she never spoke. She seemed quite oblivious to it. She did not ask to leave the villa—was content to spend each day within its confining beauty.

Meals were delivered, or concocted by them both—simple, hearty food, from salads and *charcuterie* to pasta and barbecues, prepared with much laughter and consumed with appetite. An appetite that afterwards turned to passion for each other.

I didn't know it would be like this—having Sabine with me. I didn't think it would be this...this good.

He tried to think back to a time when it had not been like this—when Sabine had not been with him, when all he'd had were his fears for Philip, his suspicions of her. But it seemed very far away—blurring in his head. Fading more and more with each hour. All that mattered to him now was being as they were now, lying side by side beneath the stars, hand in hand.

He felt her thumb move sensuously, lightly over his as their clasped hands hung loosely between them. He turned his head towards her, away from the moon above. She was gazing across at him, her face dim in the moonlight, her eyes resting on him. There was a softness in her face, in her eyes...

'Bastiaan...' Her voice was low, a sweet caress.

His eyes found hers. Desire reached into his veins. He drew her to her feet and wound his fingers into hers. Speared his hand into her hair, let his mouth find hers.

Passion, strong and sweet and true, flared at his touch. Drove them indoors to find each other, again, and yet again, in this perfect, blissful time they had together.

CHAPTER NINE

'MY *PENSION* IS just there,' Sarah said, pointing to the corner of the street. 'I won't be five minutes.'

Bastiaan pulled the car over to the kerb and she dashed inside. She wanted to change into something pretty for the day. They were finally emerging from the villa, and Bastiaan was set on taking her to a place he was amazed she hadn't seen yet.

The picturesque little town of St Paul de Vence, up in the hills behind the coastline, was famous as a place frequented by artists. She was happy enough to go there—happy enough to be anywhere in the world right now, providing Bastiaan was with her and she with him.

Bastiaan. Oh, the name soared in her head, echoed deep inside her. She was seizing all that he was holding out to her so that there was nothing else except being with him, day after precious day, night after searing night.

It's as if I were asleep and he has woken me. Woken my senses, set them alight.

In her head, in her heart, emotion hovered like a fragile bubble, iridescent and glistening with light and colour. A bubble she longed to seize but dared not—not now, not yet. But it filled her being, made her breathless with delight, with joy. Joy that brought a smile to her face now, as she ran into the *pension*, eager to be as quick as possible so she could re-join Bastiaan without delay.

Five minutes later she was running down the stairs again, pausing only to snatch at the mail in her room's pigeonhole, dropping the envelopes into her handbag before emerging out onto the roadway. She jumped into the car and off they set.

Bastiaan's gaze was warm upon her before he focussed on the way ahead.

She's changed her image yet again, he found himself thinking. This one he liked particularly, he decided. Her hair was in a long plait, her make-up no more than a touch of mascara and lip gloss, and her skin had been warmed by the sun of the past few days to a golden honey. Her outfit was a pretty floral calf-length sundress in pale blue and yellow. She looked fresh and summery and beautiful.

And *his*. Oh, most definitely, definitely his!

Emotion surged within him. What it was, he didn't know—and didn't care. Knew only that it felt good— *so* good...

The route out of the *ville* took them past the nightclub where she sang. As they drove by he saw her throw it a sideways glance, almost looking at it askance, before turning swiftly away. He was glad to have passed it too— did not want to think about it. It jarred with everything that was filling him now.

He shook his head, as if to clear it of unwelcome thoughts. At the villa, safe in its cocoon, the outside world had seemed far, far away. All that belonged in it far, far away.

Well, he would not think of it. He would think only of the day ahead of them. A day to be spent in togetherness, on an excursion, with lunch in a beautiful place, a scenic drive through the hinterland behind the coast.

The traffic lights ahead turned red and he slowed down to a halt, using the opportunity to glance at Sabine beside him. She was busying herself looking at the contents of an envelope she'd taken out of the bag on her lap. It was, he could see, a bill from the *pension*. She gave it a cursory check, replaced it in her bag, then took out another envelope. Bastiaan could see it had a French stamp on it, but she was turning it over to open it, so he could not see the writing on the front.

As she ripped it open and glanced inside she gave a little crow of pleasure. 'Oh, how sweet of him!'

Then, with a sudden biting of her lip, she hurriedly stuffed the envelope back inside her handbag, shutting it with a snap.

Abruptly the traffic lights changed, the car behind him sounded its horn impatiently, and Bastiaan had to move off. But in the few seconds that it took a chill had gone down inside him.

Had he really seen what he'd thought he'd seen?

Had that been a cheque inside that envelope?

He threw a covert sideways glance at her, but she was placing her bag in the footwell, then getting out her phone and texting someone, a happy smile playing around her mouth.

Bastiaan found he was revving the engine, his hands clenching momentarily around the steering wheel. Then, forcibly, he put the sudden burst of cold anger out of his head. Why should Sabine *not* receive mail? And if that mail were from a man what business was it of his? She might know any number of men. Very likely did…

Another emotion stabbed at him. One he had not experienced before. One he never had cause to experience. Rigorously, he pushed it aside. Refused to allow his mind to dwell on the question that was trying to make itself heard. He would *not* speculate on just who might be sending her correspondence that she regarded as 'sweet.' He would not.

He risked another sideways glance at her as he steered through the traffic. She was still on her phone, scrolling through messages. As his gaze went back to the road he heard her give a soft chuckle, start to tap a reply immediately.

Bastiaan flicked his eyes towards her phone screen, hard though it was to see it from this angle and in the brightness of the sun. In the seconds his glance took a face on the screen impinged—or did it? It was gone as she touched the screen to send her message, but he could feel his hands clenching on the wheel again.

Had that been Philip?

The thought was in his head before he could stop it. He forced it out. It had been impossible to recognise the fleeting photo. It could have been anyone. *Anyone.* He would not let his imagination run riot. His fears run riot...

Instead he would focus only on the day ahead. A leisurely drive to St Paul de Vence...strolling hand in hand through its narrow pretty streets, thronged with tourists but charming all the same. Focus only on the easy companionable rightness of having Sabine at his side, looking so lovely as she was today, turning men's heads all around and making a glow of happy possession fill him.

It would be a simple, uncomplicated day together, just like the days they'd spent together at his villa. Nothing would intrude on his happiness.

Into his head flickered the image of her glancing at the contents of that envelope in her lap. He heard again her little crow of pleasure. Saw in his mind the telltale printing on the small piece of paper she'd been looking at...

No!

He would not think about that—*he would not.*

Leave it be. It has nothing to do with you. Let your suspicions of her go—let go completely.

Resolutely he pushed it from his mind, lifting his free hand to point towards the entrance to the famous hotel where they were going to have lunch. She was delighted by it—delighted by everything. Her face alight with pleasure and happiness.

Across the table from him Sarah gazed glowingly at him. She knew every contour of his face, every expression in his eyes, every touch of his mouth upon her…

Her gaze flickered. Shadowed. There was a catch in her throat. Emerging from the villa had been like waking from a dream. Seeing the outside world all around her. Being reminded of its existence. Even just driving past the nightclub had plucked at her.

The days—the nights—she'd spent with Bastiaan had blotted out everything completely. But now—even here, sitting with people all around them—the world was pressing in upon her again. Calling time on them.

Tomorrow she must leave him. Go back to Max. Go back to being Sarah again. Emotion twisted inside her. This time with Bastiaan had been beyond amazing—it had been like nothing she had ever known. *He* was like no man she had ever known.

But what am I to him?

That was the question that shaped itself as they set off after lunch, his powerful, expensive car snaking its way back towards Cap Pierre. The question that pierced her like an arrow. She thought of how she'd assumed that a man like him would be interested only in a sophisticated seductive affair—a passionately sensual encounter with a woman like Sabine.

Was that still what she thought?

The answer blazed in her head.

I don't want it to be just that. I don't want to be just Sabine to him. I want to be the person I really am— I want to be Sarah.

But did she dare? That was what it came down to. As Sabine she had the protection of her persona—that of a woman who could deal with transient affairs…the kind a man like Bastiaan would want.

Would he still want me if I were Sarah?

Or was this burning passion, this intensity of desire, the only thing he wanted? He had said nothing of anything other than enjoying each hour with her—had not spoken of how long he wanted this to last or what it meant to him, nor anything at all of that nature.

Is this time all he wants of me?

There seemed to be a heaviness inside her, weighing her down. She stole a sideways look at Bastiaan. He was focussed on the road, which was building up with traffic now as they neared Nice. She felt her insides give a little skip as her gaze eagerly drank in his strong, incisive profile—and then there was a tearing feeling in its place.

I don't want to leave him. I don't want this to end. It's been way, way too short!

But what could she do? Nothing—that was all. Her future was mapped out for her and it did not include any more time with Bastiaan.

Who might not want to spend it with her anyway. Who might only want what they were having now. And if that were so—if all he'd wanted all along was a kind of fleeting affair with Sabine—then she must accept it.

Sabine would be able to handle a brief affair like this—so I must be Sabine still.

As Sarah she was far too vulnerable…

She took a breath, steeling herself. Her time with Bastiaan was not yet up—not quite. There was still tonight—still one more precious night together.…

And perhaps she was fearing the worst—perhaps he wanted more than this brief time.

Her thoughts raced ahead, borne on a tide of emotion that swelled out of her on wings of hope. Perhaps he would rejoice to find out she was Sarah. Would stand by her all through her final preparations for the festival—share her rejoicing if they were successful or comfort her if she failed and had to accept that she would never become the professional singer she had set her sights on being.

Like an underground fire running through the root systems of a forest, she felt emotions flare within her. What they were she dared not say. Must not give name to.

Right man—wrong time…for now…

But after the festival Bastiaan might just become someone to her who would be so much more than this incandescent brief encounter.

'Shall we stop here in Nice for a while?'

Bastiaan's voice interrupted her troubled thoughts, bringing her back to the moment.

'They have some good shops,' he said invitingly.

The dress she was wearing was pretty, but it was not a designer number by any means. Nor were any of the clothes she wore—including that over-revealing evening gown she wore to sing in. He found himself wanting to know just how a dress suitable for her beauty would enhance her. Splashing out on a wardrobe for her would be a pleasure he would enjoy. And shopping with her would keep at bay any unnecessary temptation to worry about the cheque she had exclaimed over. He would not think about it—would not harbour any suspicions.

I'm done with such suspicions. I will banish them— not let them poison me again.

But she shook her head at his suggestion. 'No, there's nothing I need,' she answered. She did not want to waste time shopping—she wanted to get back to the villa. To be with Bastiaan alone in the last few dwindling hours before she had to go.

He smiled at her indulgently. 'But much, surely, that you *want*?'

She gave a laugh. She would not spoil this last day with him by being unhappy, by letting in the world she didn't want to think about. 'What woman doesn't?' was her rejoinder.

Then, suddenly, her tone changed. Something in that world she didn't want to let in yet demanded her attention. Attention she must give it—right now.

'Oh, actually…could we stop for five minutes? Just along here? There's something I've remembered.'

Bastiaan glanced at her. She was indicating a side street off the main thoroughfare. Maybe she needed toiletries. But as he turned the car towards where she indicated, a slight frown creased his forehead. There was something familiar about the street name. He wondered why—where he had seen it recently.

Then she was pointing again. 'Just there!' she cried.

He pulled across to the pavement, looked where she was pointing, and with an icy rush cold snaked down his spine.

'I won't be a moment,' she said as she got out of the car. Her expression was smiling, untroubled. Then, with a brief wave to him, she hurried into the building.

It was a bank. And Bastiaan knew, with ice congealing in his veins, exactly which bank it was—a branch of the bank that Philip's cheque for twenty thousand euros had been paid into...

And in his head, imprinted like a laser image, he saw again the telltale shape of the contents of that envelope she'd opened in the car that morning, which had caused her to give a crow of pleasure. Another cheque that he knew with deadly certainty she was now paying into the very same account...

A single word seared across his consciousness with all the force of a dagger striking into his very guts.

Fool!

He shut his eyes, feeling cold in every cell of his body.

'All done!' Sarah's voice was bright as she got back into the low-slung car. She was glad to have completed her task—glad she'd remembered in time. But what did *not* gladden her was having had to remember to do it at all. Letting reality impose itself upon her. The reality she would be facing tomorrow...

Conflict filled her. How could she want to stay here as Sabine—with Bastiaan—when Sarah awaited her in the morning? Yet how could she bear to leave Bastiaan— walk away from him and from the bliss she had found with him? Even though all the hopes and dreams of her life were waiting for her to fulfil them...

I want them both!

The cry came from within. Making her eyes anguished. Her heart clench.

She felt the car move off and turned to gaze at Bastiaan as he drove. He'd put on dark glasses while she'd been in the bank, and for a moment—just a moment— she felt that he was someone else. He seemed preoccupied, but the traffic in the middle of Nice was bad, so she did not speak until they were well clear and heading east towards Cap Pierre.

'I can't wait to take a dip in the pool,' she said lightly. She stole a glance at him. 'Fancy a skinny-dip this time?' She spoke teasingly. She wanted to see him smile, wanted the set expression on his face to ease. Wanted her own mood, which had become drawn and aching, to lighten.

He didn't answer—only gave a brief acknowledging smile, as fleeting as it was absent, and turned off the main coastal route to take the road heading towards Pierre-les-Pins.

She let him focus on the road, her own mood strained still, and getting more so with every passing moment. Going through Pierre-les-Pins was harder still, knowing that she must be there tomorrow—her time with Bastiaan over.

Her gaze went to him as he drove. She wanted, needed, to drink him in while she could. Desire filled her, quickening in her veins as she gazed at his face in profile, wanting to reach out and touch, even though he was driving and she must not. His expression was still set and there was no casual conversation, only this strained atmosphere. As if he were feeling what she was feeling…

But how could he be? He knew nothing of what she must do tomorrow—nothing of why she must leave him, the reality she must return to.

Urgency filled her suddenly. *I have to tell him—tell him I am Sarah, not Sabine. Have to explain why…*

And she must do it tonight—of course she must. When else? Tomorrow morning she would be heading back to the *ville*, ready to resume rehearsals. How could she hide that from him? Even if he still wanted her as Sarah she could spend no more time with him now—

not with the festival so close. Not with so much work for her yet to do.

A darker thought assailed her. Did he even *want* more time with her—whether as Sarah or Sabine? Was this, for him, the last day he wanted with her? Had he done with her? Was he even now planning on telling her that their time together was over—that he was leaving France, returning to his own life in Greece?

Her eyes flickered. His features were drawn, with deep lines around his mouth, his jaw tense.

Is he getting ready to end this now?

The ache inside her intensified.

As they walked back inside the villa he caught her hand, stayed her progress. She halted, turning to him. He tossed his sunglasses aside, dropping them on a console table in the hallway. His eyes blazed at her.

Her breath caught—the intensity in his gaze stopped the air in her lungs—and then, hauling her to him, he lowered his mouth to hers with hungry, devouring passion.

She went up like dry tinder. It was a conflagration to answer his, like petrol thrown on a bonfire. Desperation was in her desire. Exultation at his desire for her.

In moments they were in the bedroom, shedding clothes, entwining limbs, passions roused, stroked and heightened in an urgency of desire to be fulfilled, slaked.

In a storm of sensation she reached the pinnacle of her arousal, hips straining to maximise his possession of her. His body was slicked with the sheen of physical ardour as her nails dug into his muscled shoulders and time after time he brought her to yet more exquisite pleasure. She cried out, as if the sensation was veering on the unbearable, so intense was her body's climax. His own was as dramatic—a great shuddering of his straining body, the cords of his neck exposed as he lifted his head, eyes blind with passion. One last eruption of their bodies and then it was over, as though a thunderstorm had passed over a mountain peak.

She lay beneath him, panting, exhausted, her conscious mind dazed and incoherent. She gazed up at him, her eyes wide with a kind of wonder that she could not comprehend. The wildness of their union, the urgency of his possession, of the response he'd summoned from her, had been almost shocking to her. Physical bliss that she had never yet experienced.

And yet she needed now, in the aftermath, to have him hold her close, to cradle her in his arms, to transform their wildness to comfort and tenderness. But as she gazed upwards she saw that there was still that blindness in his eyes.

Was he still caught there, on that mountain peak they'd reached together, stranded in the physical storm of their union? She searched his features, trying to understand, trying to still the tumult in her own breast, where her heart was only slowly climbing down from its hectic beating.

Confusion filled her—more than confusion. That same darkening, disquieting unease that had started as they'd driven back from Nice. She wanted him to say something—anything. Wanted him to wrap his arms about her, hold her as he always did after the throes of passion.

But he did no such thing. Abruptly he was pulling away from her, rising up off the bed and heading into the en-suite bathroom.

As the door closed behind him an aching, anxious feeling of bereavement filled her. Unease mixed with her confusion, with her mounting disquiet. She got out of bed, swaying a moment, her body still feeling the aftermath of what it had experienced. Her hair was still in its plait, but it was dishevelled from their passion. Absently she smoothed it with her hands. She found that they were trembling. With the same shaky motion she groped for her clothes, scattered on the floor, tangled up with his.

From the bathroom came the sound of the shower, but nothing else.

Dressed, she made her way into the kitchen. Took a drink of water from the fridge. Tried to recover her calm.

But she could not. Whatever had happened between them it was not good. How could it be?

He's ending it.

Those were the words that tolled in her brain. The only words that could make sense of how he was being. He was ending it and looking to find a way of doing so. He would not wish to wound her, hurt her. He would find an…*acceptable* way to tell her. He would probably say something about having to go back to Athens. Maybe he had other commitments she knew nothing about. Maybe…

Her thoughts were jumping all over the place, as if on a hot plate. She tried to gather them together, to come to terms with them. Then a sound impinged—her phone, ringing from inside her bag, abandoned in the hallway when Bastiaan had swept her to him.

Absently she fished it out. Saw that it was Max. Saw it go to voicemail.

She stared blindly at the phone as she listened to his message. He sounded fraught, under pressure.

'Sarah—I'm really sorry. I need you to be Sabine tonight. I can't placate Raymond any longer. Can you make it? I'm really sorry—' He rang off.

She didn't phone back. Couldn't. All she could do was start to press the keys with nerveless fingers, texting her reply. Brief, but sufficient.

OK.

But it wasn't OK. It wasn't at all.

She glanced around the kitchen, spotted a pad of paper by the phone on the wall. She crossed to it, tore off a piece and numbly wrote on it, then tucked it by the coffee machine that was spluttering coffee into the jug. She picked up her bag and went out into the hallway, looked into the bedroom. The tangled bedclothes, Bastiaan's garments on the floor, were blatant testimony to what had happened there so short a while ago.

An eternity ago.

There was no sign of Bastiaan. The shower was still running.

She had to go. Right now. Because she could not bear to stay there and have Bastiaan tell her it was over.

Slowly, with a kind of pain netting around her, her mind numb, she turned and left the villa.

Bastiaan cut the shower, seizing a towel to wrap himself in. He had to go back into the bedroom. He could delay it no longer. He didn't want to. He didn't want to see her again.

Wanted to wipe her from existence.

How could I have believed her to be innocent? How could I?

He knew the answer—knew it with shuddering emotion.

Because I wanted her to be innocent—I didn't want her to have taken Philip's money, didn't want it to be true!

That was what was tearing through him, ripping at him with sharpest talons. Ripping his illusions from him.

Fool! Fool that he had been!

He closed his eyes in blind rage. In front of his very eyes she'd waltzed into that bank in Nice, paid in whatever it was she'd taken from Philip—or another man. It didn't matter which. The same branch of that bank—the very same. A coincidence? How could it be?

A snarl sounded in his throat.

Had that cheque she'd paid in this afternoon been from Philip too? Had that postmark been from Paris? Had it been his writing on the envelope? His expression changed. The envelope would still be in her bag, even if the cheque were not. That would be all the proof he needed.

Is she hoping to take me for even more?

The thought was in his head like a dagger before he could stop it. Was that what was behind her ardency, her passion?

The passion that burns between us even now, even right to the bitter end...

Self-hatred lashed at him. How could he have done what he'd just done? Swept her to bed as he had, knowing what she truly was? But he'd been driven by an urge so strong he hadn't been able to stop himself—an urge to possess her one final time...

One final time to recapture all that they'd had—all he'd thought they'd had.

It had never been there at all.

The dagger thrust again, into the core of his being.

He wrenched open the door.

She was not there. The rumpled bed was empty. Her clothes gone.

Emotion rushed into the sudden void in his head like

air into a vacuum. But quite what the emotion was he didn't know. All he knew was that he was striding out of the room, with nothing more than a towel snaked around his hips, wondering where the hell she'd got to.

For a numb, timeless moment he just stood in the hallway, registering that her handbag was gone too, so he would not be able to check the writing on the envelope. Then, from the kitchen, he heard the sound of the coffee machine spluttering.

He walked towards it, seeing that the room was empty. Seeing the note by the coffee jug. Reading it with preternatural calm.

Bastiaan—we've had the most unforgettable time. Thank you for every moment.

It was simply signed 'S.'

That was all.

He dropped it numbly. Turned around, headed back to the bedroom. So she was walking out on him. Had the sum of money she'd extracted this time been sufficient for her to afford to be able to do so? That was what Leana had done. Cashed his cheque and headed off with her next mark, her geriatric protector, laughing at the idiot she'd fooled and left behind.

His mouth tightened. Well, things were different now. *Very* different. Sabine did not know that he was Philip's trustee, that he knew what she had taken and could learn if she'd taken yet more today. She had no reason not to think herself safe.

Is she still hoping to take more from Philip?

Memory played in his head—how Philip had asked him to loosen the purse strings of his main fund before his birthday—how evasive he'd been about what he wanted the money for. All the suspicions he'd so blindly set aside leapt again.

Grim-faced, he went to fetch his laptop.

And there it was—right in his email inbox. A communication today, direct from one of Philip's investment managers, requesting Bastiaan's approval—or not—for Philip's instruction to liquidate a particular fund. The liquidation would release over two hundred thousand euros...

Two hundred thousand euros. Enough to free Sabine for ever from warbling in a second-rate nightclub.

He slammed the laptop lid down. Fury was leaping in his throat.

Was that what Philip had texted her about? Bastiaan hadn't been mistaken in recognizing him as the sender— he could not have been. Was that why she'd given that soft, revealing chuckle? Was that why she'd bolted now, switching her allegiance back to Philip?

Rage boiled in Bastiaan's breast. Well, that would never happen—*never*! She would *never* go back to Philip.

She can burn in hell before she gets that money from him!

His lips stretched into a travesty of a smile. She thought herself safe—but Sabine Sablon was *not* safe. She was not safe at all...

And she would discover that very, very shortly.

CHAPTER TEN

SARAH REACHED FOR the second false eyelash. Glued it, like the first, with shaky hands. She was going through the motions—nothing more. Hammers seemed to be in her brain, hammering her flat. Mashing everything inside her. Misery assailed her. She shouldn't be feeling it—but she was. Oh, she was.

It was over. Her time with Bastiaan was over. A few precious days—and now this.

Reality had awaited her. Max had greeted her with relief—and apology. And with some news that had pierced the misery in her.

'This is your last night here. Raymond insisted you show up just for tonight—because it's Friday and he can't be without a singer—but from tomorrow you're officially replaced. Not with the real Sabine—someone else he's finally found. And then, thank God, we can all decamp. We've been given an earlier rehearsal spot at the festival so we can head there straight away.'

He'd said nothing else, had asked no questions. Had only cast an assessing look at her, seeing the withdrawal in her face. She was glad of it, and of the news he'd given her. Relief, as much as she could feel anything through the fog of misery encompassing her, resonated in her. Now there was only tonight to get through. How she would do it, she didn't know—but it would have to happen.

As she finished putting on her lipstick with shaky hands she could feel hope lighting inside her. Refusing to be quenched. *Was* it over? Perhaps it wasn't. Oh, perhaps Bastiaan *hadn't* been intending to end it all. Perhaps she'd feared it quite unnecessarily. Perhaps, even now, he was missing her, coming after her…

No! She couldn't afford to agonise over whether Bastiaan had finished with her. Couldn't afford to hope and dream that he hadn't. Couldn't afford even to let her mind go where it so wanted to go—to relive, hour by hour, each moment she'd spent with him.

I can't afford to want him—or miss him.

She stared at her reflection. Sabine was more alien than ever now. And as she did so, the door of her dressing room was thrust open. Her head flew round, and as her gaze fell upon the tall, dark figure standing there, her face lit, joy and relief flaring in her eyes. Bastiaan! He had come after her—he was not ending it with her! He still wanted her! Her heart soared.

But as she looked up at him she froze. There was something wrong—something wrong with his face. His eyes. The way he was standing there, dominating the small space. His face was dark, his eyes like granite. He was like nothing she had seen before. This was not the Bastiaan she knew…not Bastiaan at all…

'I have something to say to you.'

Bastiaan's voice was harsh. Hostile. His eyes were dark and veiled, as if a screen had dropped down over them.

Her heart started to hammer. That dark, veiled gaze pressed down on her. Hostility radiated from him like a force field. It felt like a physical blow. What was happening? Why was he looking at her like this? She didn't know—didn't understand.

A moment later the answer came—an answer that was incomprehensible.

'From now on stay away from Philip. It's over. Do you understand me? *Over!*' His voice was harsh, accusing. Condemning.

She didn't understand. Could only go on sitting there, staring at him, emotion surging through her chaotically. Then, as his words sank in, a frown convulsed her face.

'Philip?' she said blankly.

A rasp of a laugh—without humour, soon cut short—broke from him. 'Forgotten him already, have you? Well, then…' and now his voice took on a different note—one that seemed to chill her deep inside '…it seems my efforts were not in vain. I have succeeded, it seems, in… *distracting* you, *mademoiselle*.' He paused heavily and his eyes were stabbing at her now. 'As I intended.'

His chest rose and fell, and then he was speaking again.

'But do not flatter yourself that my….*attentions* were for any purpose other than to convince you that my cousin is no longer yours to manipulate.'

She was staring at him as if he were insane. But he would not be halted. Not now, when fury was coursing through his veins—as it had done since the veils had been ripped from his eyes—since he'd understood just how much a fool she'd made of him. Not Philip—*him!*

I so nearly fell for it—was so nearly convinced by her.

Anger burned in him. Anger at her—for taking him for a fool, for exploiting his trusting, sensitive cousin and for not being the woman he'd come to believe, to hope, that she was.

The woman I wanted her to be.

The irony of it was exquisite. He'd seduced her because he'd believed her guilty—then had no longer been able to believe that she was. Then all that had been ripped and up-ended again—back to guilt.

A guilt he no longer wanted her to have, but from which there could be no escape now. *None.*

He cut across his own perilous thoughts with a snarl. 'Don't play the innocent. If you think you can still exploit his emotional vulnerability to you…well, think again.'

His voice became harsh and ugly, his mouth curling, eyes filled with venom.

'You see, I have only to tell him how you have warmed *my* bed these last days for his infatuation to be over in an instant. Your power over him extinguished.'

The air in her lungs was like lead. His words were like blows. Her features contorted.

'Are you saying…?' She could hardly force the words from her through the pain, through the shock that had exploded inside her, 'Are you saying that you seduced me in order to…to separate me from Philip?' There was disbelief in her voice. Disbelief on so many levels.

'You have it precisely,' he said heavily, with sardonic emphasis. 'Oh, surely you did not believe I would not take action to protect my cousin from women of your kind?'

She swallowed. It was like a razor in her throat. 'My kind…?'

'Look at yourself, Sabine. A woman of the world— isn't that the phrase? Using her *talents*—' deliberately he mocked the word she'd used herself when she'd first learnt who he was '—to make her way in the world. And if those *talents*—' the mockery intensified '—include catching men with your charms, then good luck to you.' His voice hardened like the blade of a knife. 'Unless you set your sights on a vulnerable stripling like my cousin—

then I will wish you only to perdition! And ensure you go there.'

His voice changed again.

'So, do you understand the situation now? From now on content yourself with the life you have—singing cheap, tawdry songs in a cheap, tawdry club.'

His eyes blazed like coals from the pit as he gave his final vicious condemnation of her.

'A two-cent *chanteuse* with more body than voice. That is all that you are good for. Nothing else!'

One last skewering of his contemptuous gaze, one last twist of his deriding mouth, and he was turning on his heel, walking out. She could hear his footsteps—heavy, damning—falling away.

Her mouth fell open, the rush of air into her lungs choking her. Emotion convulsed her. And then, as if fuse had been lit, she jerked to her feet. She charged out of the dressing room, but he was already stepping through the door that separated the front of house from backstage. She whirled about, driven forward on the emotion boiling up inside her. A moment later she was in the wings at the side of the stage, seizing Max by the arm, propelling him forward.

Anger such as she had never felt before in her life, erupted in her. She thrust Max towards the piano beside the centre spot where her microphone was. She hurled it into the wings, then turned back to Max.

'Play "Der Hölle Rache".'

Max stared at her as if she were mad. *'What?'*

'Play it! Or I am on the next plane to London!'

She could see Bastiaan, threading his way across the dining room, moving towards the exit. The room was busy, but there was only one person she was going to sing for. Only one—and he could burn in hell!

Max's gaze followed hers and his expression changed. She saw his hands shape themselves over the opening chord, and with a last snatch of sanity took the breath she needed for herself. And then, as Max's hands crashed down on the keyboard, she stepped forward into the pool of light. Centre stage.

And launched into furious, excoriating, maximum *tessitura*, her full-powered *coloratura* soprano voice exploding into the space in front of her to find its target.

Bastiaan could see the exit—a dozen tables or so away. He had to get out of here, get into his car and drive... drive far and fast. *Very* fast.

He'd done it. He'd done what he'd had to do—what he'd set out to do from that afternoon in Athens when his aunt had come to see him, to beg him to save her precious young son from the toils of a dangerous *femme fatale*. And save him he had.

Saved more than just his cousin.

I have saved myself.

No!

He would not think that—would not accept it. Would only make for the exit.

He reached the door. Made to push it open angrily with the flat of his hand.

And then, from behind him, came a crash of chords that stopped him.

He froze.

'Der Hölle Rache.' The most fiendishly difficult soprano aria by Mozart. Fiendish for its cripplingly punishing high notes, for the merciless fury of its delivery. An aria whose music and lyrics boiled with coruscating rage as *Die Zauberflöte*'s 'Queen of the Night' poured out seething venom against her bitter enemy.

'Hell's vengeance boils in my heart!'

Like a remotely operated robot, turning against his will, Bastiaan felt his body twist.

It was impossible. Impossible that this stabbing, biting, fury of a voice should be emanating from the figure on the stage. Absolutely, totally impossible.

Because the figure on the stage was *Sabine*. Sabine—with her tight sheath of a gown, her *femme fatale* blonde allure, her low-pitched voice singing huskily through sultry cabaret numbers.

It could not be Sabine singing this most punishing, demanding pinnacle of the operatic repertoire.

But it was.

Still like a robot he walked towards the stage, dimly aware that the diners present were staring open-mouthed at this extraordinary departure from their normal cabaret fare. Dimly aware that he was sinking down at an unoccupied table in front of the stage, his eyes pinned, incredulous, on the woman singing a few metres away from him.

The full force of her raging voice stormed over him. There was no microphone to amplify her voice, but she was drowning out everything except the crashing chords of the piano accompanying her. This close, he would see the incandescent fury in her face, her flashing eyes emerald and hard. He stared—transfixed. Incredulous. Disbelieving.

Then, as the aria *furioso* reached its climax, he saw her stride to the edge of the stage, step down off it and sweep towards him. Saw her snatch up a steak knife from a place setting and, with a final, killing flourish, as her scathing, scything denunciation of her enemy was hurled from her lips, she lifted the knife up and brought it down in a deadly, vicious stab into the tabletop in front of him.

The final chords sounded and she was whirling around, striding away, slamming through the door that led backstage. And in the tabletop in front of him the knife she'd stabbed into it stood quivering.

All around him was stunned silence.

Slowly, very slowly, he reached a hand forward and withdrew the knife from the table. It took a degree of effort to do so—it had been stabbed in with driving force.

The entire audience came out of their stupor and erupted into a tremendous round of applause.

He realised he was getting to his feet, intent on following her wherever she had disappeared to, and then was aware that the pianist was lightly sprinting off the stage towards him, blocking his route.

'I wouldn't, you know,' said the pianist, whom he dimly recognised as Sabine's accompanist.

Bastiaan stared at him. 'What the *hell* just happened?' he demanded. His ears were still ringing with the power of her voice, her incredible, unbelievable voice.

Sabine's accompanist made a face. 'Whatever you said to her, she didn't like it—' he answered.

'She's a *nightclub* singer!' Bastiaan exclaimed, not hearing what the other man had said.

The accompanist shook his head. 'Ah, no…actually, she's not. She's only standing in for one right now. Sarah's real musical forte is, as you have just heard, opera.'

Bastiaan stared blankly. 'Sarah?'

'Sarah Fareham. That's her name. She's British. Her mother is French. The real Sabine did a runner, so I cut a deal with the club owner to get free rehearsal space in exchange for Sarah filling in. But he's hired a new singer now—which is very convenient as we're off tomorrow to the festival venue.'

Bastiaan's blank stare turned blanker. 'Festival…?' He

seemed to be able to do nothing but echo the other man's words, and Bastiaan had the suspicion, deep down, that the man was finding all this highly amusing.

'Yes, the Provence en Voix Festival. We—as in our company—are appearing there with a newly composed opera that I am directing. Sarah,' he informed Bastiaan, 'is our lead soprano. It's a very demanding role.' Now the amusement was not in his voice any more. 'I only hope she hasn't gone and wrecked her voice with that ridiculous "Queen of the Night" tirade she insisted on.' His mouth twisted and the humour was back in his voice, waspish though it was. 'I can't think why—can you?'

Bastiaan's eyes narrowed. It was a jibe, and he didn't like it. But that was the absolute, utter least of his emotions right now.

'I have to speak to her—'

'Uh-uh.' The pianist shook his head again. 'I really wouldn't, you know.' He made a face again. 'I have *never* seen her that angry.'

Bastiaan hardly heard him. His mind was in meltdown. And then another question reared, hitting him in the face.

'Philip—my cousin—does *he* know?'

'About Sarah? Yes, of course he does. Your cousin's been haunting this place during rehearsals. Nice kid,' said Max kindly.

Bastiaan's brows snapped together uncomprehendingly. Philip *knew* that 'Sabine' was this girl Sarah? That she was in some kind of opera company? Why the hell hadn't he told him, then? He spoke that last question aloud.

'Not surprisingly, Sarah's being a bit cagey about having to appear as Sabine,' came the answer. 'It wouldn't do her operatic reputation any good at all if it got out.

This festival is make-or-break for her. For *all* of us,' he finished tightly.

Bastiaan didn't answer. Couldn't.

She trusted Philip with the truth about herself—but she never trusted me with it!

The realisation was like a stab wound.

'I have to see her.'

He thrust his way bodily past the pianist, storming down the narrow corridor, his head reeling, trying to make sense of it all. Memory slashed through him of how he'd sought her out that first evening he'd set eyes on her. His face tightened. Lies—all damn lies.

Her dressing room door was shut, but he pushed it open. At his entrance she turned, whipping round from where she was wrenching tissues from a box on her dressing table.

'Get out!' she yelled at him.

Bastiaan stopped short. Everything he had thought he'd known about her was gone. Totally gone.

She yelled at him again. 'You heard me! Get out! Take your foul accusations and *get out*!'

Her voice was strident, her eyes blazing with the same vitriolic fury that had turned them emerald as she'd hurled her rage at him in her performance.

'Why didn't you *tell* me you weren't Sabine?' Bastiaan cut across her.

'Why didn't *you* tell *me* that you thought me some sleazy slut who was trying it on with your precious cousin?' she countered, still yelling at him.

His expression darkened. 'Of course I wasn't going to tell you that, was I? Since I was trying to separate you from him.' A ragged breath scissored his lungs. 'Look, Sabine...'

'I am *not* Sabine!'

Sarah snatched up a hairbrush from her dressing table and hurled it at him. It bounced harmlessly off his broad chest. The chest she'd clung to in ecstasy—the chest she now wanted to hammer with her fists in pure, boiling rage for what he'd said to her, what he'd thought of her...

What he'd done to her...

He took me to bed and made love to me, took me to paradise, and all along it was just a ghastly, horrible plot to blacken me in Philip's eyes.

Misery and rage boiled together in the maelstrom of her mind.

'I didn't know you weren't Sabine. Do *not* blame me for that,' Bastiaan retaliated, slashing a hand through empty air. He tried again, attempting to use her real name now. 'Look... Sarah...'

'Don't you *dare* speak my name. You know *nothing* about me!'

His expression changed. Oh, but there *was* something he knew about her. From the shredded remnants of his mind, the brainstorm consuming him, he dragged it forth. Forced it across his synapses.

She might be Sabine, she might be Sarah—it didn't matter—

'Except, of course,' he said freezingly, each word ice as he spoke it, 'about the money. Philip's money.'

She stilled. 'Money?' She echoed the word as if it were in an alien tongue.

He gave a rough laugh. Opera singer or nightclub singer—why should it be different? His mouth twisted. Why should 'Sarah' be any more scrupulous than 'Sabine'?

'You took,' he said, letting each word cut like a knife, 'twenty thousand euros from my cousin's personal account. I know you did because this afternoon you paid another cheque into the very same bank account that the twenty thousand euros disappeared into.'

Her expression was changing even as he spoke, but he wouldn't let her say anything—anything at all.

'And this very evening, after you'd oh-so-conveniently cut and run from my villa, I got a request to release *two hundred thousand* euros from my cousin's investment funds.' His eyes glittered with accusation. 'Did you not realise that as Philip's trustee I see *everything* of his finances—that he needs my approval to cash that kind of money? Running back to him with whatever sob story you're concocting will be in vain. Is *that* why you left my bed this afternoon?'

'I left,' she said, and it was as if wire were garrotting her throat, 'because I had to appear as Sabine tonight.'

She was staring at him as if from very far away. *Because I thought you'd had all you wanted from Sabine.*

And he had, hadn't he? That was the killing blow that struck her now. He'd had exactly what he'd wanted from Sabine because all he'd wanted was to separate her from Philip and to keep his money safe.

Behind the stone mask that was her face she was fracturing into a thousand pieces...

Her impassivity made him angry—the anger like ice water in his veins. 'I'll tell you how it will be,' he said. 'Philip will go back to Athens, safely out of your reach. And you—Sabine, Sarah, whoever the hell you are— will repay the twenty thousand euros that he paid into your bank account.'

Her eyes were still on him. They were as green and as hard as emeralds.

'It wasn't my bank account,' she said.

Her voice was expressionless, but something had changed in her face.

A voice came from the doorway. 'No,' it said, 'it was mine.'

CHAPTER ELEVEN

SARAH'S EYES WENT to Max, standing in the doorway.

'What the *hell* have you done?' she breathed.

He got no chance to answer. Bastiaan's eyes lasered him. 'Are you claiming the account is yours? *She* went into that bank this afternoon.'

'To pay in a cheque for three thousand euros my father had just sent me to help with the expenses of mounting the opera. I paid it directly into Max's account.'

She was looking at Bastiaan, but there was no expression in her face, none in her voice. Her gaze went back to Max.

'You took Philip for *twenty thousand euros*?' There was emotion in her voice now—disbelief and outrage.

Max lifted his hands. 'I did not ask for it, *cherie*. He offered.'

Bastiaan's eyes narrowed. Emotion was coursing through him, but right now he had only one focus. 'My cousin *offered* you twenty thousand euros?'

Max looked straight at him. 'He could see for himself how we're stretched for funding—he wanted to help.' There was no apology in his voice.

Bastiaan's eyes slashed back to Sarah. 'Did you know?'

The question bit at her like the jaws of a wolf. But it was Max who answered.

'Of course she didn't know. She'd already warned me not to approach him.'

'And yet,' said Bastiaan, with a dangerous silkiness in his voice, 'you still did.'

Max's eyes hardened. 'I told you—he offered it without prompting. Why should I have refused?' Something in his voice altered, became both defiant and accusing. 'Are we supposed to starve in the gutter to bring the world our art?'

He got no answer. The world, with or without opera in it, had just changed for Bastiaan.

His eyes went back to Sarah. Her face was like stone. Something moved within him—something that was like a lance piercing him inside—but he ignored it. He flicked his eyes back to Max, then to Sarah again.

'And the two hundred thousand euros my cousin now wishes to lavish on a fortunate recipient?' Silk over steel was in his voice.

'If he offered I would take it,' said Max bluntly. 'It would be well spent. Better than on the pointless toys that rich men squander their wealth on,' he said, and there was a dry bitterness in his words as he spoke.

'Except—' Sarah's voice cut in '—that is exactly what Philip is planning to do.'

She opened a drawer in the vanity unit, drew out her phone, called up a text, pointed the screen towards Bastiaan.

'This is the text he sent me today, while we were driving to St Paul de Vence.' Her voice was hollow.

His eyes went to it. Went to a photo of the latest supercar to have been launched—one of those he and Philip had discussed over dinner in Villeneuve.

The accompanying text was simple.

Wouldn't this make a great twenty-first birthday present to myself? I can't wait!

Underneath, he could read what she had replied.

Very impressive! What does Bastiaan think? Check with him first!

Sarah was speaking. 'I was as tactful as I could be—I always have been. I don't want him hurt, whatever he thinks he feels about me, but I never wanted to encourage him. And not about this, either,' she replied, in the same distant, hollow voice. 'I know you're not keen on him having such a powerful car so young.'

Harsh realisation washed through Bastiaan like a chilling douche. Philip had been so evasive about why he wanted money released from his funds...

But it wasn't for her—none of the money was for her...

And she was not, and never had been, the person he'd thought her...not in any respect whatsoever. Neither nightclub singer, nor gold-digger, nor any threat at all, in any way, to Philip.

My every accusation has been false. And because of that...

His mind stopped. It was as if he were standing at the edge of a high cliff. One more step forward and he would be over the edge. Falling to his doom.

Sarah was getting to her feet. It was hard, because she seemed to be made of marble. Nothing seemed to be working inside her at all. Not in her body, not in her head. She looked at Bastiaan, at the man she'd thought he was. But he wasn't. He was someone quite different.

'You'd better go,' she said. 'My set starts soon.' She

paused. Then, 'Stay away from me,' she said. 'Stay away—and go to hell.'

From the doorway, Max tried to speak. 'Sarah...'

There was uncertainty in his voice, but she just looked at him. He gave a slight shrug, then walked away. Her eyes went back to Bastiaan, but now there was hatred in them. Raw hatred.

'Go to hell,' she said again.

But there was no need to tell him that. He was there already.

He turned and went.

Sarah stood for one long motionless, agonising, end-less moment, her whole body pulled by wires of agony and rage. Then tears started to choke her. Tears of fury. Tears of misery.

Aching, ravening misery.

His aunt was staring at him from across her drawing room in Athens. Bastiaan had just had lunch with her and Philip, and now, with Philip back at his studies, his aunt was cornering him about his mission to the Riviera.

'Bastiaan, are you telling me that this girl in France is actually some sort of opera singer and *isn't* trying to entrap Philip?'

He nodded tautly.

His aunt's expression cleared. 'But that's wonderful.' Then she looked worried. 'Do you think he's still... *enamoured*, though? Even if she isn't encouraging him?'

He shook his head. 'I don't think so. He's full of this invitation to go to the Caribbean with Jean-Paul and his family.' He cast his aunt a significant look. 'Plus, he seems to be very taken with Jean-Paul's sister, whose birthday party it is.'

Philip's mother's face lit. 'Oh, Christine is a sweet

girl. They'd be so well-suited.' She cast a grateful look
at her nephew. 'Bastiaan—*thank you*. I cannot tell you
how grateful I am for setting my mind at rest about that
singer and my boy!'

His eyes were veiled for a moment, and there was a
fleeting look that he hid swiftly. His expression changed.
'I made one mistake, though,' he said.

More than one...

His throat closed, but he forced himself to continue.
'I let Philip drive my car while we were there—now he's
determined to get one of his own.'

His aunt's face was spiked with anxiety. 'Oh,
Bastiaan—please, stop him. He'll kill himself!'

He heard the fear in her voice, but this time he shook
his head. 'I can't stop him—and nor can you. He's grow-
ing up. He has to learn responsibility. But—' he held up
a hand '—I *can* teach him to drive a car like that safely.
That's the deal I've struck with him.'

'Well...' her acquiescence was uneasy, but resigned
'...if you do your best to keep him safe...'

'I will,' he said.

He got to his feet. He needed to be out of there. Needed
it badly. He was heading off to his island, craving soli-
tude. Craving anything that might stop him thinking.
Stop him feeling...

No—don't go there. Just...don't.

As he walked towards the front door Philip hailed
him from his room. 'Bast! You will come, won't you?
To Sarah's premiere? It would be so great if you do. You
only ever saw her as Sabine—she'd love you to see what
she can really do. I know she would.'

His eyes veiled. What Sarah would love was to see
his head on a plate.

'I'll see,' he temporised.

'It's at the end of next week,' Philip reminded him.

It could be tomorrow or at the end of eternity for all the difference it would make, Bastiaan knew. Knew from her brutal, persistent refusal to acknowledge any of his texts, his emails, his letters. All of them asking... *begging* one thing and one thing only...

His mind sheered away—the way he was training it to. Day by gruelling day. But it kept coming back—like a falcon circling for prey. He could sail, he could swim, he could walk, he could get very, very drunk—but it would not stay out of his head.

Three simple words. Three words that were like knife-thrusts to his guts.

I've lost her.

'Sarah?'

Max's voice was cautious. It wasn't just because of the thorny issue of Philip's generosity and Max's ready acceptance. He was treating her with kid gloves. She wished he wouldn't. She wished he would go back to being the waspish, slave-driving Max she knew. Wished that everyone would stop tiptoeing around her.

It was as if she had a visible knife wound in her. But nothing was visible. Her bleeding was internal...

It was their first rehearsal day at the festival site, a small but beautiful theatre built in the grounds of a château in northern Provence. She was grateful—abjectly grateful—to be away from the Riviera...away from the nightclub. Away from anything, everything, that might remind her of what had happened there...

But it was with her day and night, asleep and awake, alone and with others, singing or not.

Pain. A simple word. Agonizing to endure.

Impossible to stop.

'Are you sure you want to start with that aria?' Max's enquiry was still cautious. 'Wouldn't you rather build up to it?'

'No,' she said.

Her tone was flat, inexpressive. She wanted to do this. Needed to do it. The aria that she had found impossible to sing was now the only one she wanted to sing.

She took her position, readied herself—her stance, her throat, her muscles, her breathing. Anton started to play. As she stood motionless, until her entry came, thoughts flowed through her head…ribbons of pain…

How could I not understand this aria? How could I think it impossible to believe in it—believe in what she feels, what she endures?

Her bar came. Max lifted his hand to guide her in as the music swelled on its pitiless tide. She gazed blindly outward, not seeing Max, not seeing the auditorium or the world. Seeing only her pain.

And out of her pain came the pain of the War Bride, her anguished voice reaching out over the world with the pain of hopes destroyed, happiness extinguished, the future gone. The futility, the loss, the courage, the sacrifice, the pity of war…all in a single voice. *Her* voice.

As her voice died away into silence…utter silence… Anton lifted his hands from the keyboard. Then he got to his feet, crossed to her. Took her hands. Kissed each of them.

'You have sung what I have written,' he told her, his voice full. It was all he said—all he needed to say.

She shut her eyes. Inside her head, words came. Fierce. Searing.

This is all I have. And it will be enough. It will be enough!

But in the deepest recesses of her consciousness she could hear a single word mocking her.

Liar.

Bastiaan took his seat. He was up in the gods. He'd never in his life sat so high above the stage, in so cheap a seat. But he needed to be somewhere where Philip, down in the stalls, could not see him.

Bastiaan had told him that, regrettably, he could not make it to the opening night of *War Bride.*

He had lied.

What he did not want—could not afford—was for Philip to let Sarah know he would be there.

But he could no more have stayed away than remained in a burning building.

Emotion roiled within him as he gazed down. Somewhere behind those heavy curtains she was there. Urgency burned in him. She had blocked him at every turn, denied him all access.

Even Max, when he'd asked for his intervention, had simply replied, 'Sarah needs to work now. Don't make any more difficulties for her.'

So he'd stayed away. Till now.

Tonight—tonight I have to speak to her. I have to.

As the house lights went down and the audience started to settle, conversation dimming, he felt his vision blur. Saw images shape themselves—tantalizing, tormenting.

Sabine, her eyes glowing with passion, gazing up at him as they made love.

Sabine, smiling, laughing, holding his hand.

Sabine—just being with her, hour by hour, day by day, as they ate, as they swam, as they sunbathed and star-gazed.

Sabine—so beautiful, so wonderful.

Until I threw her away.

He had let fear and suspicion poison what they'd had. Ruin it.

I did not know what I had—until I lost it.

Could he win it back? Could he win *her* back?

He had to try—at least he had to try.

'OK, Sarah, this is it.' Max was pressing his hands on her shoulders, his eyes holding hers. 'You can do it—you know you can.'

She couldn't respond, could only wait while he spoke to the others, reassuring them, encouraging them. He looked impeccable in white tie and tails, but she could see the tension in him in every line of his slight body. She could hear the audience starting to applaud and the tuning up of the players in the orchestra die away as Max, their conductor for the evening, took the podium.

She tried to breathe, but couldn't. She wanted to die. Anything—anything at all to avoid having to do what she was going to have to do. What she had been preparing for all her life. What she had worked for in every waking second, allowing nothing else to lay claim to an instant of her time, a moment of her concentration.

Least of all the man who had done what he had to her. Least of all him. The man who was despicable beyond all men, thinking what he had of her, judging and condemning her as he had, while all the while…all the while…

He made love to me and thought me nothing better than a cheap little gold-digger. Right from the start— from the very moment he laid eyes on me. Everything was a lie—everything! Every moment I spent with him was a lie. And he knew it the whole time!

No, she had not allowed such vicious, agonizing thoughts into her head. Not one. She'd kept them all at bay—along with all those unbearable texts and voice-mails that she'd deleted without reading or listening to. Deleted and destroyed, telling him to go to hell and stay there. Never, ever to get in touch again.

Because all there was in her life now was her voice—her voice and her work. She had worked like a demon, like one possessed, and blocked out everything else in the universe. And now this moment, right now, had come. And she wanted to die.

Dear God, please let me do OK. Please let me get it right—for me, for all of us. Please.

Then the small chorus was filing out on to the stage, and a moment later she heard Max start the brief overture. She felt faint with nerves. As they took their places the familiar music, every note of which she knew in every cell of her body, started to wind its way through the synapses of her stricken brain. The curtain rose, revealing the cavern of the auditorium beyond, and now the chorus was starting their low, haunting chant—their invocation to vanishing peace as the storm clouds of war gathered.

She felt her legs tremble, turning to jelly. Her voice had gone. Completely gone. Vanished into the ether. There was nothing—nothing in her but silence...

She saw the glare of the stage lights, the dimness of the auditorium beyond, and on his podium Max, lifting his baton for her entrance cue. She fixed her eyes on him, took a breath.

And her voice came.

High and pure and true. And nothing else in the universe existed any more except her voice.

Unseen, high above in the gods, Bastiaan sat motionless and heard her sing.

The knife in his guts twisted with every note she sang.

For the whole duration of the opera, as it wound to its sombre conclusion, Bastiaan could not move a muscle, his whole being riveted on the slender figure on the stage. Only once did he stir, his expression changing. During the heartrending aria of grief for her young husband's death, with the agony of loss in every note. His eyes shadowed. The poignancy of the music, of her high, keening voice, struck deep within him.

Then the drama moved on to its final scene, to her song to the unborn child she carried, destined to be another soldier, in yet another war. And she, the War Bride, would become in her turn the Soldier's Mother, destined to bury her son, comfort his widow—the next War Bride, carrying the next unborn soldier...

As her voice faded the light on the stage faded too, until there was only a single narrow spot upon her. And then that, too, faded, leaving only the unseen chorus to close the timeless tragedy with a chorale of mourning for lives yet to be lost in future conflicts. Until silence and darkness fell completely.

For a palpable moment there was complete stillness in the house—and then the applause started. And it did not stop. Did not stop as the stage lights came up and the cast were there, Sarah, and the other soloists stepping forward. The applause intensified and the audience were rising to their feet as Max walked out on to the stage with Anton at his side, and then both of them were taking Sarah by the hand, leading her forward to a crescendo of applause.

Bastiaan's palms were stinging, but still the applause continued, and still his eyes were only for her— for Sarah—now dropping hands with Max, calling her tenor forward, and the other soloists too, to take their share of the ovation, breaking the line to let the chorus take theirs, and then all the cast joined in with applause for the orchestra taking their bows.

He could see her expression—beatific, transfigured.

He could stay still no longer. He rose from his seat, jolted down the staircase to the ground floor, out into the fresh night air. His heart was pounding, but not from exertion. Walking swiftly, purposefully, he pushed open the stage door, walked up to the concierge's booth.

'This is for Max Defarge. See that he gets it this evening.' He placed the long white envelope he'd taken from his inside jacket pocket into his hand, along with a hundred-euro note to ensure his instruction was fulfilled. Then he walked away.

He couldn't do this. What the hell had he been thinking? That he could just swan into her dressing room the way he had that first night he'd seen her sing?

Seen Sabine sing—not Sarah!

But the woman he'd heard tonight had not been Sabine—had been as distant from Sabine as he was from the stars in the sky. That knife twisted in his guts again, the irony like acid in his veins. That he should now crave only the woman he had thrown away....distrusted and destroyed.

His mobile phone vibrated. Absently he took it out—it was a text from Philip.

Bast, you missed a sensation! Sarah was brilliant and the audience is going wild! Gutted you aren't here. Am staying for the after-party soon as the audience clears. Can't wait to hug her!

He didn't answer, just slid the phone away. His heart as heavy as lead.

CHAPTER TWELVE

SARAH WAS FLOATING at least six inches off the ground. The champagne that Max had splashed out on was contributing, she knew, but mostly it was just on wings of elation—the buoyancy of abject relief and gratitude that she had given the performance of her life.

Elation filled them all—hugs and kisses, tears and laughter and joy lifting them all above the exhaustion that their efforts had exacted from them. But no one cared about exhaustion now—only about triumph.

She could scarcely believe it, and yet it was true. All true. Finally all true.

'Am I dreaming this?' she cried to her parents as they swept her into their arms. Her mother's face was openly wet with tears, her father's glowing with pride.

Her mother's hand pressed hers. 'Whoever he is, my darling—the man you sang about—he's not worthy of you.' Her voice was rich with sympathy and concern.

Sarah would not meet her mother's eyes.

Her mother smiled sadly. 'I heard it in your voice. You were not singing of the loss of your soldier. It was real for you, my darling—*real*.'

Sarah tried to shake her head, but failed. Tried to stop the knife sliding into her heart, but failed. She could only be grateful that Max was now embracing her—for the millionth time—and drawing her off to one side. He found a quiet spot in the foyer area where the after-party was taking place and spoke.

'This has just been given to me,' he said.

His voice was neutral. Very neutral. Out of his pocket he took a folded piece of paper and opened it, handing it to Sarah. She took it with a slight frown of puzzlement. Then her expression changed.

'I'm glad for you,' she said tightly. It was all she could manage. She thrust the paper back at Max.

'And for yourself?' The question came with a lift of the brow, speculation in his eyes, concern in his voice.

She gave her head a sharp, negative shake. Turned away bleakly. Heading back into the throng, she seized up another glass of champagne, more hugs, more kisses. And suddenly, a huge bear hug enveloping her.

'Oh, Sarah… Sarah—you were brilliant. Just *brilliant*! You were *all* brilliant!'

It was Philip—sweet, lovely Philip—his face alight with pleasure for her. She hugged him back, glad to see him. But automatically, fearfully, she found her gaze going past him. And there was another emotion in her eyes—one she did not want to be there but which leapt all the same.

It died away as he spoke again. 'I just *wish* Bast could've been here. I told him I really, *really* wanted him to hear you do your real stuff—not all that inane Sabine garbage.' He released her from his hug.

She smiled fondly. 'Thank you for all your loyalty and support. It means a great deal to me,' she said sincerely, because his youthful faith in her had, she knew, been a balm to her. 'And Philip?' She pressed his hands, her voice serious now. 'Listen—don't *ever* let types like Max take money off you again. He was out of order.'

He coloured again. 'I wanted to help,' he said.

For a second, just a second, her eyes shadowed with pain. Philip's 'help' had exacted a price from her and she had paid heavily. Was still paying.

Would pay all her life...

'You did,' she said firmly. 'And we're all grateful—you helped make all this possible!' She gestured widely at the happy scene around them.

'Great!' He grinned, relieved and reassured.

She, too, was relieved and reassured. Philip's crush on her was clearly over, there was no light of longing in his eyes any more. Just open friendliness. 'We all liked you hanging around—with or without that hefty donation to us. Oh, and Philip?' Her face was expressive. 'That monster car you want to get for yourself—please, just do *not* smash yourself up in it!'

He grinned again. 'I won't. Bast's teaching me to drive it safely.' He blew her a kiss as he headed off. 'One day I'll deliver you to the artists' entrance at the Royal Opera House Covent Garden in it—see if I don't.'

'I'll hold you to that,' she said fondly.

She turned away. Covent Garden... Would she make it there? Was what had happened tonight the first step on her journey there?

Fierce emotion fired through her.

I have to make it. I have to!

Work and work alone must consume her now. No more distractions.

The words echoed in her head, mocking her. How often had she said them?

Even right from the start, when her eyes had set on the man who had invaded her dressing room that night, invaded her life...

Invaded my heart...

She felt a choke rising in her throat, constricting her breathing. She forced it back. She would not give in to it. Would not give in to the bleakness that was like a vacuum inside her, trying to suck all the joy out of this moment for her.

My work will be enough—it will be!

That was all she had to remember. All she had to believe.

Lie though it was…

An hour later she had had enough of celebration. The exhaustion she'd blanked out was seeping through her again.

Her parents had gone, yawning, back to their hotel in the nearby spa town. Philip was getting stuck into the champagne with the chorus, with a lot of laughter and bonhomie.

Helping herself to a large glass of water, Sarah found her feet going towards the French windows. Cool fresh air beckoned her, and she stepped out onto a paved area. There was an ornate stone-rimmed pond at the end of a pathway leading across the lawn, with soft underwater lights and a little fountain playing. She felt herself wandering towards it.

Her elation had gone. Subsumed not just by exhaustion but by another mood. Seeing Philip had not helped her. Nor had what Max had disclosed to her. Both had been painful reminders of the man she wanted now only to forget.

But could not.

She reached the pond, trailed her fingers in the cool water, her gaze inward. Back into memory.

Sun sparkling off the swimming pool as Bastiaan dived into it, his torso glistening with diamond drops of water.

His arm tight around her as he steered the motorboat towards the gold of the setting sun. His eyes burning down at her with passion and desire. His mouth, lowering to hers...

She gave a little cry of pain. It had meant nothing—nothing to him at all. False—all false!

Bitter irony twisted inside her.

I thought he wanted me to be Sabine—a woman of the world, alluring and sensual, willing and eager for an instant romance. But all along Sabine was the woman he wanted to destroy.

And destroy her he had.

Too late she had discovered, after a few brief, fleeting days of passion and desire, how much more she wanted. Wanted as Sarah—not Sabine.

Pain shot through her again. And too late she had discovered what she was to Bastiaan...what she had been all along, through every kiss, every caress, every moment she'd spent with him.

Discovered that she had lost what she had never had at all.

The choke rose in her throat again, but she forced it back. She would not weep, would not shed tears. She snatched her hand from the water, twisted around, away from the stone pond.

And looked straight at Bastiaan.

He walked towards her. There was a numbness in him, but he kept on walking. She stood poised, motionless, looking so achingly beautiful, with her gold hair coiled at her nape, her slender body wreathed in an evening gown of pale green chiffon.

As he drew closer, memory flashed. The two of them sitting behind the wheel of his boat, moving gently on the low swell of the sea, her leaning into him, his arm around her waist, as he turned its nose into the path of the setting sun, whose golden rays had burnished them as if in blessing.

Another memory, like a strobe light, of them lying together, all passion spent, during the hours of the night, her slender body cradled in his. Another flash, and a memory of the fragrance of fresh coffee, warm croissants, the morning sun reaching its fingers into the vine-shaded terrace as they took their breakfast.

Each memory became more precious with every passing hour.

Each one was lost because of him. Because of what he'd done to her.

He could not take his eyes from her. Within him emotion swelled, wanting to overtake him, to impel him to do what he longed to do—sweep her into his arms. He could not—dared not. Everything rested on this moment—he had one chance…one only.

A chance he must take. Must not run from as he had thought to do, unable to confront her in the throng inside, at the moment of her triumph in her art. But now as she stood there, alone, he must brave the moment. Reclaim what he had thrown from him—what he had not known he had possessed.

But I did know. I knew it with every kiss, every embrace, every smile. I knew it in my blood, my body—my heart.

As he came up to her, her chin lifted. Her face was a mask. 'What are you doing here? Philip said you weren't here. Why did you come?'

Her words were staccato. Cold. Her eyes hard in the dim light.

'You must know why I am here,' he said. His voice was low. Intense.

'No. I don't.' Still staccato, still that mask on her face. 'Is it to see if I'm impressed by what you've done for Max? All that lavish sponsorship! Is it by way of apology for your foul accusations at me?'

He gave a brief, negating shake of his head and would have spoken, but she forged on, not letting him speak.

'Good. Because if you want to sponsor him—well, you've got enough money and to spare, haven't you? I want none of it—just like I never wanted Philip's.' She took a heaving breath, 'And just like I want nothing more to do with you either.'

He shut his eyes, receiving her words like a blow. Then his eyes flared open again. 'I ask only five minutes of your time, Sab—Sarah.'

He cursed himself. He had so nearly called her by the name she did not bear. Memory stabbed at him—how he had wondered why Philip stammered over her name.

If I had known then the truth about her—if I had known it was not she who had taken money from Philip...

But he hadn't known.

He dragged his focus back. What use were regrets about the past? None. Only the future counted now—the future he was staking this moment on.

She wasn't moving—not a muscle—and he must take that for consent.

'Please...please understand the reasons for my behaviour.'

He took a ragged breath, as if to get his thoughts in order. It was vital, crucial that he get this right. He had one chance...one chance only...

'When Philip's father died I promised his mother I would always look out for him. I knew only too well that he could be taken advantage of. How much he would become a target for unscrupulous people.'

He saw her face tighten, knew she was thinking of what Max had done, however noble a cause he'd considered it.

He ploughed on. 'Especially,' he said, looking at her without flinching, 'women.'

'Gold-diggers,' she said. There was no expression in her voice.

'Yes. A cliché, but true all the same.'

A frown creased between Bastiaan's eyes. He had to make her understand what the danger had been—how real it could have been.

If she had truly been the woman I feared she was.

'I know,' he said, and his mouth gave a caustic curl of self-derision, 'because when I was little older than Philip, and like him had no father to teach me better, a woman took me to the cleaners and made a complete fool of me.'

Did he see something change in her eyes? He didn't know—could only keep going.

'So when I saw that twenty thousand euros had gone from Philip's account to an unknown account in Nice... when I heard from Paulette that Philip had taken to hanging around a nightclub endlessly and was clearly besotted with someone, alarm bells rang. I *knew* the danger to him.'

'And so you did what you did. I know—I was on the receiving end.'

There was bitterness in her voice, and accusation. She'd had enough of this—*enough.* What was the point of him going on at her like this? There wasn't one. And it was hell—just hell on earth—to stand here with him so close, so incredibly close.

So unutterably distant… Because how could he be anything else?

She made herself say the words that proved it. 'I get the picture, Bastiaan. You seduced me to safeguard Philip. That was the only reason.' There was a vice around her throat, but she forced the words through.

She started to turn away. That vice around her throat was squeezing the air from her. She had to get out of here. Hadn't Bastiaan Karavalas done enough to her without jeopardizing everything she had worked to achieve?

'*No.*'

The single word, cutting through the air, silenced her.

'No,' he said again. He took a step towards her. 'It was not the only reason.'

There was a vehemence in the way he spoke that stilled her. His eyes were no longer veiled…they were burning—burning with an intensity she had never seen before.

'From the moment I first saw you I desired you. Could not resist you even though I thought you were Sabine, out to exploit my cousin. *Because* I thought that it gave me…' he took a breath '…a justification for doing what I wanted to do all along. Indulge my desire for you. A desire that you returned—I could see that in every glance you gave me. I knew you wanted me.'

'And you used that for your own ends.' The bitterness was back in her voice.

He seemed to flinch, but then he was reaching for her wrist to stay her, desperate for her to hear what he must say—*must* say.

'I regret everything I did, Sarah.' He said her name with difficulty, for it was hard—so hard—not to call her by the name he'd called her when she was in his arms. 'Everything. But not—not the time we had together.'

She strained away from him. 'It was fake, Bastiaan. Totally fake.' There was harshness in her voice.

'Fake?' Something changed in his voice. His eyes. His fingers around her wrist softened. 'Fake...?' he said again.

And now there was a timbre to his voice that she had heard before—heard a hundred times before...a thousand. She felt a susurration go through her as subtle as a breath of wind in her hair. As caressing as a summer breeze.

'Was *this* fake?' he said,

And now he was drawing her towards him and she could not hold back. The pulse in her veins was whispering, quickening. She felt her breath catch, dissolve.

'Was *this* fake?' he said again.

And now she was so close to him, so close that her head was dropping back. She could catch the scent of his body, the warmth of it. She felt her eyes flutter shut and then he was kissing her, the softness of his lips a homage, an invocation.

He held her close, and closer still, cupping her nape to deepen his kiss.

Bliss eased through her, melting and dissolving. Dissolving the hard, bitter knot of pain and anger deep inside her. He let her lips go, but his eyes were pouring into hers.

'Forgive me—I beg you to forgive me.' His voice was husky, imploring. 'I wronged you—treated you hideously. But when I made those accusations at you—oh, they were tearing me to pieces. To have spent those days with you, transforming everything in my life, and then that final day...' He shut his eyes, as if to shut out the memory, before forcing himself to open them again, to speak to her of what had haunted him. 'To think myself duped—

because how could you be that woman I'd feared you were when what we had was so…so wonderful.'

His voice dropped.

'I believed all my fears—and I believed the worst fear of all. That you were not the woman I had so wanted you to be…'

He gazed down at her now, his hand around her nape, cradling her head, his eyes eloquent with meaning. And from his lips came the words he had come here to say.

'The woman I love—Sabine or Sarah—*you* are the woman I love. Only you.'

She heard the words, heard them close, as close as her heart—the heart that was swelling in her breast as if it must surely become her very being, encompassing all that she was, all that she could be.

She pressed her hand against the strong wall of his chest, glorying in feeling her fingers splay out over the hard muscle beneath his shirt. Feeling the heat of his body, the beat of his heart beneath her palm.

Wonder filled her, and a whitening of the soul that bleached from her all that she had felt till now—all the anger and the hurt, the fury and the pain. Leaving nothing but whitest, purest bliss.

She gazed up at him, her face transformed. He felt his heart turn over in his breast, exultation in it.

'I thought it impossible…' she breathed. 'Impossible that in a few brief days I could fall in love. How could it be so swift? But it was true—and oh, Bastiaan, it hurt so *much* that you thought so ill of me after what we'd had together.'

To love so swiftly—to hurt so badly…

She saw him flinch, as if her words had made a wound, but he answered her.

'The moment I knew—that hellish moment when I knew everything I'd feared about you, all I'd accused you of was false…nothing but false… I knew that I had destroyed everything between us. You threw me out and I could do nothing but go. Accept that you wanted nothing to do with me. Let you get on with your preparations for tonight without my plaguing you.'

His voice changed. 'But tonight I could keep silent no longer. I determined to find you—face you.' A rueful look entered his dark eyes. 'I bottled it. I was too… too scared to face you.' His gaze changed again, becoming searching. 'What you've achieved tonight—what it will bring you now—will there be room for me? *Can* there be?'

She gave a little cry. 'Oh, Bastiaan, don't you see? It's *because* of what I feel—because now I know what love is—that I can achieve what I have tonight…what will be in me from now for ever.'

She drew back a little.

'That aria I sang, where the War Bride mourns her husband's death…' She swallowed, gazing up at him with all her heart in her eyes. 'She sings of love that is lost, love that burns so briefly and then was gone. I couldn't sing it. I didn't understand it until—'

He pulled her into his arms, wrapping them tight around her. 'Oh, my beloved, you will *never* feel that way again. Whatever lessons in love you learn from me will be happy ones from now. Only happy ones.'

She felt tears come then, prickling in her eyes, dusting her lashes with diamonds in the starlight. Bastiaan—*hers*. Her Bastiaan! After such torment, such bliss! After such fears, such trust. After such anger, such love…

She lifted her head to his, sought his mouth and found

it, and into her kiss she poured all that was in her heart, all that she was, all that she would be.

An eternal duet of love that they would sing together all their lives.

EPILOGUE

SARAH LAY ON the little sandy beach, gazing up at the stars which shone like a glittering celestial tiara overhead. There was no sound but the lapping of water, the night song of the cicadas from the vegetation in the gardens behind. But her heart was singing—singing with a joy, a happiness so true, so profound, that she could still scarcely credit it.

'Do you remember,' the low, deep voice beside her asked, 'how we gazed up at the stars by the pool in my villa at Cap Pierre?'

She squeezed the hand that was holding hers as she and Bastiaan lay side by side, their eyes fixed on eternity, ablaze overnight in the Greek sky.

'Was it then?' she breathed. 'Then that I started to fall in love with you?'

'And I with you?'

Her fingers tightened on his. Love had come so swiftly she had not imagined it possible. And hurt had followed.

But the pain I felt was proof of love—it showed me my own heart.

Now all that pain was gone—vanished and banished, never to return! Now, here with Bastiaan, as they lay side by side on the first night of their married life together, they were sealing their love for ever. He had asked her where she wanted to spend her honeymoon but she had seen in his eyes that he already knew where he wanted them to be.

'I always said,' he told her, 'that I would bring my bride to my island—that she alone would be the one woman I would ever want here with me.'

She lifted his hand to her mouth, grazing his knuckles with a kiss.

'I also always said—' and his voice was different now, rueful and wry '—that I would know who that woman would be the moment I set eyes on her.'

She laughed. She could do that now—now that all the pain from the way he had mistrusted and misused her was gone.

'How blind I was! Blind to everything that you truly were! Except…' And now he hefted himself on to one elbow, rolled on to his hip to gaze down at her—his beloved Sarah, his beloved bride, his beloved wife for all the years to come. 'Except to my desire for you.'

His eyes blazed with ardour and she felt her blood quicken in its veins as it always did when he looked at her like that, felt her bones melting into the sand beneath her.

'That alone was true and real! I desired you then and I desire you now—it will never end, my beautiful, beloved Sarah!'

For an instant longer his gaze poured into hers, and then his mouth was tasting hers and she was drawing him down to her. Passion flared and burned.

Then, abruptly, Sarah held him off. 'Bastiaan Karavalas—if you think I am going to spend my wedding night and consummate my marriage on a beach, with pebbles digging into me and sand getting into places I don't even want to think about, then you are—'

'Entirely right?' he finished hopefully, humour curving his mouth.

'Don't tempt me,' she said huskily, feeling her resolve weaken even as she started to melt again.

But you do tempt me...

The words were in Bastiaan's head, echoing hers, taking him back—back to the time when he had been so, so wrong about her. And so, so right about how much he wanted her. He felt his breath catch with the wonder of it all. The happiness and joy that blazed in him now.

He got to his feet, crouched beside her, and with an effortless sweep scooped her up into his arms. She gave a little gasp and her arms went around his neck, clinging to him.

'No,' he said firmly, 'you're right. We need a bed. A large, comfortable bed. And, as it happens, I happen to have one nearby.'

He carried her across the garden into the house behind. It was much simpler than the villa in Cap Pierre, but its privacy was absolute.

The grand wedding in Athens a few hours ago, thronged with family and friends, with Sarah's parents, his aunt and his young cousin—Philip having been delighted at the news of their union—and even his own mother, flown in from LA, seemed a world away.

Max had delivered Sarah fresh from rehearsals for a production of *Cavalleria Rusticana*—with himself directing and Sarah singing 'Santuzza' at a prestigious provincial opera house in Germany—making it very clear to her that the only reason he was tolerating her absence was because she happened to be marrying an extremely wealthy and extremely generous patron of the opera, whose continued financial sponsorship he fully intended to retain.

'Keep the honeymoon short and sweet!' Max had ordered her. 'With your career taking off, it has to come first!'

She'd nodded, but had secretly disagreed. Her art and her love would always be co-equal. Her life now would be hectic, no doubt about that, and future engagements were already being booked up beyond her dreams, but they would never—*could* never—displace the one person who for all her life would stand centre stage to her existence.

She gazed up at him now, love blazing in her eyes, as he carried her into the bedroom and lowered her gently upon the bed, himself with her.

'How much…' he said huskily, this man she loved. 'How much I love you…'

She lifted her mouth to his and slowly, sweetly, passionately and possessively, they started together on their journey to the future.

* * * * *

*If you enjoyed this story,
check out these other great reads from
Julia James.*

CAPTIVATED BY THE GREEK
THE FORBIDDEN TOUCH OF SANGUARDO
SECURING THE GREEK'S LEGACY
PAINTED THE OTHER WOMAN
THE DARK SIDE OF DESIRE

Available now!

#3437 WEDDED, BEDDED, BETRAYED
Wedlocked!
by Michelle Smart
When Elena Ricci is kidnapped by Gabriele Mantegna, she never expects her body to ignite with Gabriele's every touch! As the chemistry that blazes as brightly as their hatred builds, will it lead to a legacy that will last a lifetime?

#3438 EXPECTING A ROYAL SCANDAL
Wedlocked!
by Caitlin Crews
For Felipe Cairo to avoid the shackles of duty, he must choose a *most* inappropriate wife, and Brittany Hollis has an unrivaled reputation. Until a twist shocks them *both*...Brittany might not be queen material, but she's carrying a royal heir!

#3439 SIGNED OVER TO SANTINO
by Maya Blake
Three years after sharing one night of oblivion with Javier Santino, Carla Nardozzi needs his help! The Spanish aristocrat seizes his chance for revenge on the only woman to walk away from *him*— Carla must become his lover!

#3440 THE SURPRISE CONTI CHILD
The Legendary Conti Brothers
by Tara Pammi
After nearly losing her life, Alexis Sharpe determines to tell Leandro Conti about their child. Leandro regrets how he treated Alexis seven years ago, but now that she's back and the mother of his child, he will claim *everything* that's his!

"Mistress," Nikolai slotted in, cool as ice.

Shock had welded Ella's tongue to the roof of her mouth because he was sexually propositioning her and nothing could have prepared her for that. She wasn't drop-dead gorgeous...*he* was! Male heads didn't swivel when Ella walked down the street because she had neither the length of leg nor the curves usually deemed necessary to attract such attention. Why on earth could he be making *her* such an offer?

"But we don't even know each other," she said dazedly. "You're a stranger..."

"If you live with me I won't be a stranger for long," Nikolai pointed out with monumental calm.

And the very sound of that inhuman calm and cool forced her to flip around and settle distraught eyes on his lean, darkly handsome face.

"You can't be serious about this!"

"I assure you that I am deadly serious. Move in and I'll forget your family's debts."

"But it's a *crazy* idea!" she gasped.

"It's not crazy to me," Nikolai asserted. "When I want anything, I go after it hard and fast."

Her lashes dipped. Did he want her like that? Enough to track her down, buy up her father's debts, and try to buy rights to her and her body along with those debts? The very idea of that made her dizzy and plunged her brain into even greater turmoil. "It's immoral... It's blackmail."

"It's definitely *not* blackmail. I'm giving you the benefit of a choice you didn't have before I came through that door," Nikolai Drakos fielded with glittering cool. "That choice is yours to make."

"Like hell it is!" Ella fired back. "It's a complete cheat of a supposed offer!"

Nikolai sent her a gleaming sideways glance. "No, the real cheat was you kissing me the way you did last year and then saying no and acting as if I had grossly insulted you," he murmured with lethal quietness.

"You *did* insult me!" Ella flung back, her cheeks hot as fire while she wondered if her refusal that night had started off this whole chain reaction. What else could possibly be driving him?

Nikolai straightened lazily as he opened the door. "If you take offence that easily, maybe it's just as well that the answer is no."

Don't miss
BOUGHT FOR THE GREEK'S REVENGE
by Lynne Graham,
available June 2016 wherever
Harlequin Presents® books and ebooks are sold.

www.Harlequin.com